<u>Letting Go</u>

Maria E. Monteiro

To Erika
Congratulation
on winning
With all my love

Maria E Monteiro

Copyright © 2012 by Maria E. Monteiro

Cover Design by Jen Naumann

Cover Image by Shutterstock.com

Rebel Road Publishing 2012
New York

ISBN: 978-0-9853481-2-0 (ebook)
ISBN: 13:978-1481214384 (print)
ISBN: 10:1481214381 (print)

Find Maria E. Monteiro Online:

www.MariaMonteiro.net

http://twitter.com/Mmonteiro33

http://www.FaceBook.com/RebelRoadBooks

Also available by Maria E. Monteiro:

Hold on Tight

Acknowledgements

First I like to thank my mother, who continues to support all of my dreams with all she has. I owe everything to her. I also like to thank my husband, who sits and listens to all my crazy ideas, and always makes me feel like I'm the most special person in the world. A very special thank you to my father and brother, who although have never read anything I wrote still mange to support me one hundred percent.

To my best friend Jeanette, you are one of the most important persons in my life. I thank you for always being there no matter what is going on in your life. I love you. You're my rock. Another special thank you to Dana, Joie, and Lorraine. You guys always make me feel like I'm part of your family and I will never to be able to thank you enough for all your support.

Lidia, you know you rock. Thank you so much for everything and always reading everything I sent you. You know how much I value your opinion and advice. Pat, Priscilla and Karen, you guys are not only my co-workers but also my family. I love each and every one of you.

To Bern, thank you so much for being my editor. You hold a very special place in my heart, and I will always thank you for inspiring me to go after my dream. To the rest of my family, who in their own way show their support for me, thank you. And a big thank you to Jen Naumann, who has become a true friend. I never in my life thought I would form a friendship like this with someone I've yet to meet in person. Trust me one day we will meet. Thank you for being there for all my rants, tears, and cheers. You really are an amazing friend.

Dedicated to:

My mother, who has also become my best friend.

Table of Content

1
<u>I'm Not Okay (I Promise)</u>

I sprint down the stairs gripping Nash's black hoody and the manila envelope containing the portrait he drew of me in my hands. I might finally be ready to forgive him. Then again, maybe I shouldn't, especially after he used me in his ploy to get revenge on Court.

Nash hurt me in a way no one else ever has. In spite of all this, I can't stop thinking about him. I wish I had a callous heart so I wouldn't be in love with him.

Even so, how can I start something with him again if I don't fully trust him? My mind is a jumble of thoughts. I wish I knew what to do. Hopefully this weekend in the Hamptons will help me decide what I really want. Maybe I'll get a sign that will lead me in the right direction.

I open my front door and step out into the bright sunlight. My right hand, immediately reacts, shielding my eyes from the sun that seems to be trying to blind me. The Tiffany bracelet Court gave me dances in rays of gold. I hate to admit it, but I'm happy it's back on my wrist.

"Come on. We gotta go if we wanna avoid the traffic," Court says with his magical smile that somehow still can make my heart race.

13

"I'm coming." I continue to walk towards him, but stop when I hear the humming of a motor. I know this sound all too well—it's Nash's motorcycle.

He pulls in on his blue Harley Davidson right behind Court's Mercedes. A rush of panic envelops my body. What is he doing here? What does he want? I quickly glance over to Court and notice his perfect smile vanishes as his eyes fill with anger.

My parents step out of the car looking as confused as I feel. My father takes a step towards Nash, but stops when my mother grabs his arm. She must also know I have to talk to him.

Nash hops off his motorcycle, removes his helmet that releases his dirty blond hair to the soft wind that has suddenly arrived to cool down the unforgiving heat. He begins to walk towards me with his golden green eyes, which the sun is causing to look more golden than green, glued on me. He doesn't even turn his head to acknowledge my parents or Court. Every step he takes towards me, makes my heart pound through my chest. My fingers tighten their hold on his sweatshirt.

"What are you doing here?"

"I had to see you before you left. There is so much I need to tell you. Do you think we can go somewhere and talk?" Nash says. The heat from his body almost burns through mine.

"Yes, but I can't right now." I motion over to Court's car with my eyes.

"Then when?"

"When I get back."

"Okay, but there's something I have to do before you leave." He quickly steps closer, and without any hesitation, he takes me into his arms and begins to kiss me in front of my parents and Court.

His soft tender lips feel perfect pressed against mine. I close my eyes and begin to kiss him back. It feels so good to be once again in his arms. It doesn't even matter that we have an audience. This is what I needed from him; to show me that he really does love me, and I wasn't just some pathetic pawn for him.

A smell seemingly overpowers my nose as cool salty drops of water land on my sunburned skin. I try to open my eyes but the sun forces them shut. What's happening?

My heart quickly goes from beating fast to a free fall, as I begin to realize, I'm not in my driveway with Nash. Instead I'm on the beach with hundreds of strangers. It was all an apparent dream.

The ocean mist hits my body repeatedly, fully livening my senses. I raise my fingers to my lips tasting sand and salt. I still can't believe it was all a dream. That kiss felt so real—I wish it had been real.

Nash did not show up at my house the day I left for the Hamptons. Instead, he sent me a text, hours after I had arrived. His first text has been the pinnacle moment of this whole trip so far.

I was lying on my bed wishing I had stayed home, when my phone buzzed with his text. The words "**I miss u**" lit up my phone screen. Tears filled my eyes as my stomach twirled with excitement.

Without even thinking about it, I texted him right back and have been texting him ever since. We mostly talk about unimportant things. I told him from the start, I didn't want to discuss our relationship until we see each other face to face.

I find myself waiting for his messages all day long. They have become my escape from this place. I thought coming to the Hamptons would be the perfect getaway I needed, but it hasn't been.

As beautiful as this place is, I'm not happy being here. To begin with, the Hamptons stand for everything I hate. People around here show off their wealth by the size of their homes, the cars they drive, and the labels they wear. It's totally the opposite of who I am.

I'm not the type of girl who carries her bag on her forearm, so everyone can see the label, or wear shoes with red soles to indicate I've spent way too much money for them. I prefer my black canvas bag and my Converse sneakers.

I'm not the only one that doesn't like this place. My father also hates it here. He says it reminds him of everything he doesn't have. He's been spending a lot of the time on the beach with me.

My mother, on the other hand, is really enjoying herself. She even let Mrs. Dobberson give her a makeover. She came home after shopping with her, with a new haircut. Her hair is no longer past her shoulders; it's now cut into a picture-perfect bob with golden highlights. She also had on a new outfit, which included a pastel pink sweater set, to fit perfectly with her new hair. I thought she looked just as beautiful as Mrs. Dobberson, but she no longer looked like my mother. Gone was her hippie flare, which I love so much.

My father looked impressed at first, but then became concerned about how much it all cost. My mother just reminded him we only live once and she wants to live this life looking as good as she can. If only she would realize she looked good just the way she was. This place seems to have had a bad influence on her.

There is one more reason it's been hard to be here. Court's mother no longer is a fan of mine. She invited my parents for the weekend, but didn't realize I was coming too. I think she only invited me because she thought I wouldn't have the guts to show up.

Mrs. Dobberson is no longer the sweet woman I met at the beginning of summer. She blames me for her son getting into a fight, which resulted in his getting a black eye and being suspended from Fairland Park.

She really hasn't said much to me besides, "Oh, I didn't know you were joining us too." My mother and Court think I'm imagining it, but I can tell she no longer is fond of me. For this reason, I have tried my best to just stay on the beach and away from their house as much as I can.

Court has stayed by my side for most of the time. I feel bad, because I know he would rather be doing other things, like hanging out with his friends. They are not happy I'm monopolizing all his time. I think they might be starting to dislike me more than they already do.

I haven't told Court that Nash has contacted me. I don't want him to get mad. I just got him back in my life again and I don't want to lose him. I like our friendship and I really hope it continues even if I decide to give Nash another chance.

I also haven't told Nash that I'm down here with Court. He believes I went away with my parents somewhere further upstate. I'll tell him the truth after we have our talk. I don't want the same drama we had this summer before we even get the chance to decide what we want to do.

"There you are," Court says startling me and bringing me back to reality.

"How's Adam?"

"Heart broken. I told him not to get involved with his brother's girlfriend. I knew it was going to end up messy," he says sitting next to me on my black and purple striped beach towel. He scoops a handful of sand in his hand and watches it slowly slip through his fingers.

"Sounds messy. If you wanna go hang out with him tonight, it's ok. I was planning on staying in and reading anyway."

"On our last night here? I don't think so. Besides, I already have plans for us."

"Please don't tell me we're going to another party." In the last three nights we've been to over five parties. I think I can live the rest of my life without going to another party in the Hamptons again. I'd rather go to one of Leo's gatherings with a bonfire and a local band playing.

"Nothing like that. My brothers are heading over to their friend's houses and our parents are going to a party."

"So what are we doing?" I ask leaning back on my arms, as I look out towards the distant horizon, which is overcome by purple and pink streaks.

"We are staying in and having a special dinner."

"Just you and me?"

"Yeah, just you and me. So what do you say? Or, we could always tag along with our parents to another party."

"I think dinner sounds perfect." I get up and wipe the sand from my skin that has glued itself onto me.

As I grab my phone, I notice I have a new text from Nash. It must have arrived while I was talking to Court. I really want to read it now, but I can't do it in front of him. "I need to go take a shower and stuff. How about I meet you in an hour?"

"Perfect."

I turn around and run towards his huge house that's almost as big as his mansion back in Cypress Oak. I run through the door and up the white painted stairs skipping every other step. I don't stop running until I'm in what has been my bedroom for the last three nights.

I close the curtains on the three windows that are directly across from the door. I don't know why I feel like I need complete privacy to read his message. I sit on my queen-size bed, which is adorned with a white feather down comforter, and take a deep breath before I wake my phone from standby to unlock the screen. My stomach drops as I begin to read it.

* * *

I know I was wrong, for at first only dating Emma to get back at Court, but along the way, I really did fall in love with her. And after a while it stopped being about getting back at Court and more about being with Emma.

She was able to wake up a part of me again, after feeling numb for so long, following the death of my brother. She made me want to live again and really believe in myself. But then it all got screwed up when Angie revealed my stupid plan to her.

That day I lost everything. I wanted to punch myself in the face for hurting her. Instead, Court punched me when we got into a fistfight over it. I walked out of work feeling empty again.

I knew I had lost Emma forever. I decided to quit my job at Fairland Park, to not cause her any more pain. Giving her up was one of the hardest things I've ever had to do. Then I saw her with Court at the ice-cream stand and knew I couldn't stay away much longer.

The next day, I drove to her house to speak to her, only to have her run away. I chased her down and finally convinced her to listen to me. I poured my heart out in the rain hoping she would forgive me and maybe give me another chance. After saying everything I wanted her to know, I took a risk and kissed her. She actually kissed me back, but seconds later she pushed me away again.

Emma thought I was still using her to get back at Court. She left me standing in the rain with a broken heart. Once again I thought of giving up, until Leo convinced me to go after what I want.

I sucked up my pride and went to apologize to Court. Let's just say he didn't take it as well as I thought he would. He warned me to stay away from Emma. I lied to him and told him I would.

Instead, I went home and drew a portrait of her. Then I wrote on the back of it how much I loved her and how I would not give up on her. At two in the morning, I drove to her house and left it in her mailbox hoping it would have some kind of impact on her.

When I didn't hear from her, I texted her and was happy when she texted me right back. She said we could talk on Tuesday when she comes back from where ever she happens to be. I can't wait.

I've tried to find out where she is, but neither Britney nor Roxy would tell me. I'm just glad she's not with Court.

"Yo! You here to help or just stand around?" Leo asks putting the kegs down by the wooden stairs that lead up to his house.

"Whatever. I got all the wires set for the stage. What time is the band getting here?"

"Now," Leo says pointing to the guys from the band Louder Drift, who are walking out of his house. "People should be arriving any minute. So get this shit done already."

"Okay, just remind me next year to say no when you ask me to help you." Leo begins to laugh. I really don't mind setting up for his Labor Day party, especially knowing tomorrow at this time Emma will hopefully be in my arms again.

Leo's backyard fills up quickly with people I know and people I've never seen before. Everyone is drinking and eating while they dance around to the first song Louder Drift is singing.

Leo has a very strict policy on drinking and driving, so he makes everyone promise they'll camp out in his backyard if they drink. By the looks of it, his backyard is going to be full with sleeping bags tonight.

I'm personally not in the mood to drink. I want to have a clear head when I see Emma tomorrow. Besides, I'd rather eat since I haven't had anything since this morning.

I head to the grill stopping every so often to talk to people I know. If I continue like this, I'm going to get to the grill when all the burgers are gone. I'm starving.

I spot Roxy and Britney talking by the grill with their backs to me. The devious side of decides I'm going to take this chance to scare the shit out of Roxy. I start to walk slowly towards them hoping they don't hear me. I reach my hand out to grab her, but stop when I hear her say Emma's name.

"I wonder if Emma is having a good time in the Hamptons." *So that's where Emma is.*

"She's texted me a couple of times. I think she's having fun," Britney says, right before she takes a sip of her drink.

"Do you think she's hooked up with Court yet? It's the perfect place to do it." What the hell did she say?

"I hope so."

"What did you say?" I ask, interrupting their conversation and surprising both of them. "Is Emma with Court right now?"

"It's not really any of your business. But if you must know, yes she is. You need to move on and leave her alone," Britney says snapping her gum.

I'm a stupid fool for thinking that Emma wanted to be with me again. "This is bullshit." I begin to walk away with a hot head and a chest full of anger.

"Nash!" I hear Roxy yell, but I don't turn around. Instead, I pull my phone out and text Emma, "**I know where ur & who ur with. I won't bother u anymore.**" I turn my phone off and head towards the kegs. I really need a drink now.

I grab a plastic cup and fill it to the rim. I chug it down in one gulp and fill my cup again. As the sun begins to set, I continue to drink and drink. I need to get rid of this pain I'm in.

After an hour of trying to drown my sorrows, I try to get up for another cup of beer and fall back down. I'm starting to regret drinking without eating anything. I can feel the alcohol begin to mess with my head and work my stomach.

The non-existing food wants to exit my sour stomach. I need to get into Leo's house and away from all this. I begin to walk towards Leo's house. I try my best to walk in a straight line, but I can't. I wobble to left and then to the right. Each step is harder than the prior one.

I reach the stairs happy I didn't bang into anyone. With my legs trembling I look up at the wooden stairs. How the hell am I going to go up there without busting my ass? I take the first step and wobble just a little. Damn my head is spinning. I take another step holding on to the railing for dear life. I continue to climb, and before I know it I manage to climb the stairs without falling.

Once inside, I fall back onto Leo's plaid couch and close my eyes. I wish my head would stop spinning. It's nice to be away from all that noise. Wow, it's been a really long time since I've drunk this much.

With my eyes closed, all I can see is Emma.

Emma with Court.

Emma kissing Court.

Emma doing other things with Court.

I really think I'm going to be sick now. A loud thump jars my head. I can't even open my eyes to see who walked in. I hope whoever it is, gets what they need and gets the hell out.

"What are you doing in here all by yourself?" a familiar voice asks. I open my eyes just in time to see Angie come to kneel in front of me. Her black hair loosely falls down covering her breasts that are trying their best to stay in her bra and not pop out of her white low cut tank top. I can't deal with this right now.

"What do you want?"

"To talk to you. Don't you wanna talk to me?"

"I'm not in the mood," I say closing my eyes again. Why won't this room stop spinning?

"We don't have to talk. There are other things we could do?" She begins to move her hands up my legs.

I push her hands away. But she quickly guides them back and begins to move them higher up my leg. I jump up before my body can respond to her soft touch.

23

She jolts up and blocks me from walking towards the door. "Move!"

"Don't you miss me?"

"No. Leave me alone!"

"Are you gonna hate me forever?"

"Maybe."

"Oh come on Nash, don't you remember how happy we were together?" She strokes a strand of hair from my face. Her fingertips feel so good on my boozed-numb skin.

She gets closer. I can smell a sweet jasmine-vanilla scent coming from her. She wraps her arms around my neck. "Don't you miss me even a little?" I don't know if it's the beer, but I find myself nodding.

"I miss you too. Nash, you and I belong together. Can't you see that?"

I don't respond and I don't push her away either. I don't have the energy.

Her breath glides across my neck giving me tingles that are also making a certain part of my anatomy stand at attention. She looks at me with her deep chocolate brown eyes, which together with the alcohol, are working against what I know is right. She leans forward and begins to kiss me. My eyes close and I immediately start thinking about Emma kissing Court the same way Angie is kissing me. Anger fills me again and I begin to kiss her back.

I need this kiss to erase all the pain I'm feeling. I grab the back of Angie's head and bring her in closer. I engulf her mouth with mine. Her tongue wanders into my mouth playfully looking for mine.

Why isn't this working?

Why is Emma still the only one I can think of?

Reality snaps me back and hits me like a brick in the face. This isn't right. I let go of Angie and push her away. "No. This is a mistake."

"The only mistake is that we are not together."

She places her hands lovingly on my face and tries to kiss me again, but I pull away just in time.

"I said no."

"Why not? Is it because of that bitch?"

"It's becau…." My attention quickly shifts past Angie towards Britney who is now standing in the doorway texting on her phone. Fuck!

2
All Falls Down

My stomach churns with trepidation. How can I be so close to working things out with Nash, only to lose everything again? Why didn't I just tell him the truth? I'm so stupid.

I dial his number as fast as my fingers can tap the touch screen. I need to tell him it's not what he thinks. I know once he knows the truth, he'll understand. He just has to understand.

His voicemail comes on after only one ring. I take a deep breath in and begin to explain everything, "Nash, you need to know it's not what you think. Yes, I'm in the Hamptons with Court, but I'm not here with him in that way. I came here with my parents to stay at his house as friends. I would still like to see you tomorrow. Text me if you still want to talk." I hope to God he still wants to.

I lay back on the bed holding my phone as tears build up in my eyes. I really need him to respond. Please phone buzz. Please!

Footsteps in the hallway interrupt my thoughts. My parents must be on their way out. Please let them leave without stopping at my door. I'm not in the mood to see them.

The footsteps stop right in front of my door. "Emma?" My mother says gently knocking on my door.

"Yeah." I know if I don't say anything, she'll just open my door. I don't understand why every room I seem to sleep in never has a lock.

"We're leaving."

"Okay. Have a good time."

"Is everything okay?"

"Yeah, just getting ready for dinner with Court," I lie, trying to disguise my heartache.

"Okay. Have a good time." I hear some mumbling, which I'm sure is my father rushing her out. Her footsteps trail off leaving me alone in comforting silence once again.

Why isn't Nash texting me back? I dial his number again, but once again it goes straight to voicemail. I try calling Britney hoping she can find him and help him realize it's not what he thinks, but she doesn't answer either.

I'll just text her instead, "**Please do me a favor. Find Nash & ask him 2 call me.**" Hopefully she'll do it. I know she doesn't really like him after he hurt me.

BBBUUUZZZZZ! I spring off the bed not knowing what to do with myself. I'm so scared to see what it says. What if he doesn't want to talk to me anymore?

I slowly pick up my phone raising it to see the delivered message and with one eye open I read, "**Dinner is ready.**" The message is from Court. I can't stop the disappointment from filling every essence of my being. I totally forgot I had to meet him downstairs. All I want to do is stay in my room and be miserable, but I can't do that to Court.

I get up and quickly wash my face. I put on a pair of cut off jeans and my old CBGB black tank top, which my mother keeps begging me to throw away because it's so old. I bought it at a thrift store and it has been my comfort shirt ever since.

I decide to leave my phone behind. I don't want to take it down with me, or I'll spend the whole dinner worrying about getting a text. Why did I even agree to dinner? I wonder if Court will get mad if I cancel?

As soon as I walk into the dining room, I realize it's too late to cancel. The cherry-wood dining table is dressed in its best with candles placed on square shaped mirrors, and baby breath flowers in mason jars line the table. I swear it looks like it came straight out of a Martha Stewart magazine.

I'm starting to regret what I chose to wear. Why didn't I wear one of the dresses my mother brought for me for this trip? For the first time ever, I feel like my tank top is better off in the garbage.

"Do you like?" Court asks with his perfect smile that always warms my heart. He looks so handsome in his khaki cargo shorts and button down green and white striped shirt. His wet hair hangs in front of his eyes making him somehow look hotter than he is.

I raise my left hand up to tuck my hair behind my left ear, but stop midway when I remember he knows I do this when I'm nervous. "It's beautiful. I can't believe you did all this."

"Actually our moms helped."

"Did your mother know it was me who was gonna have dinner with you?"

"Yeah. Will you stop thinking she doesn't like you. She does. Trust me."

"If you say so." I wish I could believe that, but I know deep down Mrs. Dobberson knows I'm the reason her baby boy was hurting so much this summer.

"So what are we eating?" I ask sitting at one end of the very long table. Please don't let it be anything too extravagant. My stomach does not do fancy food.

Court comes to sit right next to me. "You'll see."

Seconds later Luis, the family's chef, comes in carrying two plates with silver dome covers on them. I'm really scared to see what's under them. Luis picks up the cover and reveals a cheeseburger with the works and shoestring fries. My body relaxes as my stomach prepares to receive some yummy food. This might be just what my broken heart needs.

I take one bite and am in pure heaven. The cheddar cheese combines with onions, pickles, tomato, lettuce, and some special sauce I've never tasted before, blend into a party in my mouth. I think this might be the best burger I have ever eaten.

"I love to see you smile," Court says staring at me.

"Food always makes me happy."

"I really like that about you."

"What?" I ask stuffing fries into my mouth.

"That you're not afraid to eat. So many girls I know are always so worried about what they put in their mouths. You and maybe Rebecca are the only girls I know that don't mind eating in front of guys."

I had forgotten about Court's friend Rebecca who worked with him on The Mind Twister. I remember the first time I ever met her, she took pleasure in bumping very hard into me. I guess you could just add her name to the long list of people who don't like me.

"I like food and I'm not ashamed of it. I'm also happy you're not scared of eating in front of a girl." We both begin to laugh. I'm really glad I didn't cancel on him. I needed this to get my mind off what Nash must be making up in his head.

For the next ninety minutes we talk about all of the memories we've shared in the short time we've been in each other's lives. Many times stopping because we're laughing so hard. We don't speak about our break up, or mention Nash.

I have been trying hard not to think about him, but I do. As much as I'm laughing and smiling, inside I'm suffering. I really wish Nash had not found out I was here until I was able to explain it to him. I need to go up to my room to check my phone.

"Thank you for dinner. It was perfect," I say as I shove the last couple of fries into my mouth.

"Please don't tell me you're ready to call it a night," Court says giving me his famous puppy eyes. I swear he can get me to do anything with that look.

"Of course not. So what do you wanna do next?" I need to come up with an excuse to go up to my room to check my phone.

"How about we go for a walk and get some ice cream."

"Court Dobberson, you know me so well. Sounds like a plan. But first let me run up to get a sweatshirt."

"Okay. I'll meet you at the door in ten minutes."

"Okay." I run up to my room and sink into Nash's sweatshirt. Just being in it makes me feel closer to him again.

With my fingers crossed, I walk towards my phone on the bed. Please let there be a message. I pick it up and feel my heart start thumping faster, when I notice I have one text message waiting for my attention. As quick as my heart started to speed up, it returns to its normal pace when I see it's from Britney. It's a picture.

I click on it to download and wait to see what she's sent me. It's probably a picture of someone doing something stupid at Leo's party. No matter how much fun I'm having with Court, I would give anything to be there.

The picture finally comes in and a sinking sick sensation comes over me. I was right, she did capture someone doing something stupid. Right there on my phone is a picture of Nash kissing Angie with the words "**Just thought u should know. Nash is an ASSHOLE!**"

I look at the picture again hoping to see Angie kissing Nash, and him trying to pull away, but it's not like that. His hands are on the back of her head as he pulls her in closer for a deeper kiss. I know that move all too well; he's used it on me many times in the past when he was trying to convince me he actually had feelings for me.

Tears fall freely down my face. I can't believe what a fool I continue to be. I can't believe I was going to give him another chance.

Something comes over me and I begin to wipe away my tears. I'm tired of crying over Nash Harrison. I'm tired of hurting. I take off his sweatshirt and throw it into a plastic bag. I'm done.

* * *

I storm out of Leo's house looking for Britney. That girl is fast; she's disappeared into the crowd before I can spot her. I can't believe this. I really hope she didn't see anything. And if she did, it had better not be Emma who she was texting.

Somehow my body has sobered up. I have no trouble walking among all the people this time. I've never seen this many people at one of Leo's parties before. Where did they all come from?

I walk all over Leo's huge backyard but I can't find her, it's like she disappeared into thin air. Where can she be?

As I walk back towards the stairs, I spot Sam by one of the Kegs. He has to know where she is. I march towards him as my patience is starting to run out. I need to find this girl now. I know she doesn't like me and will do anything to ruin any chance I have with Emma.

"Where the hell is Britney?"

"I don't know. Why?" Sam asks after taking a sip of his beer.

"I need to talk to her."

"About what?"

"Do you know where the hell she is or not?"

"First tell me why you're looking for her."

I close my eyes, take a very deep breath in, and try my best to keep my anger out of my voice. "I really need to talk to her. Just tell me where she is."

"About what?"

"Sam, I ain't playing this game with you."

He nervously fingers his jet-black hair back and says. "Maybe you shouldn't talk to her right now. Actually, I rather you don't. Not when you're like this."

"Sam!" Before I can say anything else, I see Britney walking toward us with a sly smile on her face. Damn it!

"What's going on?" She asks, sliding right next to Sam.

"I need to talk to you." I try my best to sound nice.

"What do you want?"

"Look, what you saw earlier is not what you think."

"Oh, so you weren't kissing Angie?"

"I was, but it's not what you think." I try explaining, feeling like I'm begging her to understand. Every muscle in my body tenses with anger. "Look, did you text Emma about what you saw or not?"

"Maybe," She wittingly responds crossing her arms under her chest as she tilts her head to the side. "Lets just say she saw exactly what I saw."

My blood begins to boil. I can't believe she would do this. "YOU"RE A FUCKIN' BITCH!" I yell, walking towards her.

"HEY!" Sam yells stepping in front of me as Britney steps back appearing scared. Sam's black eyes look as if they want to kill me. I've never seen him this mad before. "Don't you ever talk to my girl like that! Or you'll be dealing with me! Do you understand?" I know he's trying to be brave in front of his idiot girlfriend. I can feel him shaking in his sneakers. I don't want to start any shit with him right now.

I turn around and begin to walk towards my truck. I'm so stupid. Why did I let Angie kiss me? And why the hell did I kiss her back? If Emma didn't hate me before, I'm sure she does now. I need to get out of here.

"Where are you going?" Leo calls running after me.

"Home!" I don't turn to face him. I keep walking towards my truck that is parked in front of his house.

He runs past me, and positions himself in such a way that prevents me from going any further. "I can't let you leave."

"Why not?"

"Cause you've been drinking. You know our rule, we don't get behind the wheel if we've been drinking. Don't be an ass, give me your keys."

"I'm fine. I have to get out of here, just let me go."

"I swear if I have to kick your ass to keep you here, I will." Why does he have to make this so difficult? Can't he see I'm not drunk anymore? Who am I kidding? I couldn't walk a straight line if you paid me.

"I'll drive him home," a voice from behind me calls out. I turn around and see Angie walking towards us. What does she want now? Her tank top seems to have shrunken even more in the last hour. "I haven't had anything to drink. I can drive him home."

Leo raises one eyebrow and gives me a weary look.

I know if I don't agree to let her drive me, Leo won't let me leave, and right now, all I want to do is go home and be alone. "It's fine." I toss my keys towards Angie, who now is smiling as if she won some sort of battle.

"Are you sure?" Leo asks still looking uncertain.

"Yeah. I'll call you tomorrow."

"Don't worry, I'll make sure he gets home safe," Angie says getting in the driver side. I hop in my truck, lean back, and close my eyes. I wonder how Emma is feeling.

3
Under a Paper Moon

I walk back down the stairs feeling like a huge fool. All I want to do is erase Nash from my life. I wish I'd never met him; all he's done is bring me pain.

"You ready for some ice cream?" Court asks, meeting me by the front door.

"How about we just go for a walk instead?"

"You're not in the mood for ice cream? Are you okay?"

"Yeah. I'm just still full from dinner."

"No problem. Hey, where's your sweatshirt?"

"I decided I no longer want it."

As soon as I step outside, I take a deep breath and try to let the scent of the ocean calm me down. I'm going to have to do everything I can to keep it together. I can't fall apart in front of Court.

We begin to walk towards the beach, and seconds later, have our feet buried in the cold sand. The beach is so beautiful at night with the full moon reflecting across the waves.

The sand, on the other hand, feels so dense tonight, or maybe that's just my heart. Each step feels heavier than the one before. By the time we get to the shore, my legs feel worn out.

From afar, I can hear all the parties going on. I wonder if Court would rather be at one of those parties, than here with me. God knows, I'm not great company right now.

"Are you sure you're alright."

"Yeah," I say trying my best to give him a big smile.

He nods as he looks at me skeptically.

We continue to walk without saying one word, just listening to the waves as they crash to shore. I'm trying my best not to think about what I just saw up in my room. I hate Nash. Why did he do this to me again?

"Are you sure you're okay?" Court asks again stopping short to face me.

"Yeah. It's just the sand in my sneakers." I take them off and immediately begin to squeeze the cold grains of sand between my toes. Court takes my sneakers from me, and holds them in one hand while simultaneously grabbing my hand with the other. His touch is the perfect cure for my broken heart.

We begin to walk again in silence, only giving each other side-glances accompanied by smiles. It's weird how comfortable it can be, not to say anything. Why didn't I pick Court? I would be so happy right now if I would've just stayed with him.

"Are you okay with your brother Aaron going to private school instead of Cypress Oak High School?" I ask, stopping to glance out at the ocean.

"Nah. I mean I'm going to miss him, but I'm happy for him." He laughs shaking his head. "Can you believe we'll be back in school in a couple of days?"

"I know. This summer went by too fast. I guess it was all the fun we were having at Fairland Park."

"Yeah, right."

"Are you gonna tell me you didn't have fun watching all those strangers scream their heads off on The Mind Twister?"

"Oh yeah, tons of fun." He laughs, but then stops and with seriousness in his voice he says, "Sometimes I wish I would have made you trade with me, and I would've worked in the arcade. Then things might have ended differently. This summer really did not turn out the way I thought it would."

"Because of me." I whisper. "I'm really sorry. I wish...."

"No, I'm sorry." He turns to look at me. "I shouldn't have brought it up."

"You must hate me."

"No, that's just it, I don't hate you. I hate the situation we're in."

"What situation?"

"Being out here with you and feeling things I shouldn't. Wanting to do things I know I can't." His eyes fill with agony.

My breathing becomes little spasms of nervousness. He wants to do something he can't. A part of me wants him to do it too.

"What are you thinking about?" He asks.

"That I'm happy to be out here with you."

He smiles.

"And that maybe I want you to do what you can't."

Court comes closer, closing the space between us. The cool air makes my body shiver; at least I think it's the cool air. His eyes glow in the moonlit night.

His face starts to come towards mine, as my heart begins to thump louder and louder. The smell of his cologne makes my insides go wild. At this moment, there's no one else in this world but us. I close my eyes and wait for his lips to reach mine. I need him to kiss me.

I take another small breath, as I wait for his lips to press against mine. I continue to wait, but nothing happens. Why hasn't he kissed me yet? I open one eye, and see he's just staring at me. His eyes are no longer glowing, but look conflicted instead. He's not going to kiss me.

He's not going to…oh screw it. I lean forward and begin to kiss him. His sweet lips send chills throughout my whole body. I had forgotten how good it felt to have his lips on mine. Once again, why didn't I pick him?

He takes his strong arms and wraps them around my waist. My body becomes Jello in his embrace. I need to forget the image that is not only burning the screen on my cell phone, but also my brain.

His arms squeeze me tight, while his tongue dances in my mouth, and I return by following my tongue back into his. I am helplessly losing myself in this moment.

"I've really missed kissing you," Court says with his lips still pressed against mine.

"Me too." I continue to delight in his lips. I don't want it to stop until Nash is fully removed from my being.

"Get a room!" A couple of kids yell.

I begin to laugh, as I pull away. I look up at Court and notice he doesn't seem to think it's as funny as I do. Instead he looks perplexed. He steps further away and murmurs, "I shouldn't have kissed you."

"Actually, I kissed you." I utter, while clumsily twisting my hands together.

"Then I shouldn't have kissed you back. It was a big mistake." Each word coming out of his mouth is like tiny paper cuts going across my heart causing me horrible pain.

Rejected twice in one night is becoming too much for me to handle right now. My emotions explode and tears emerge from my eyes before I can stop them. I don't want Court to see me cry. I quickly lower my head and sob, "I'm sorry." I turn around and run away before he has a chance to respond.

I run faster than I've ever run before. My legs and lungs are quickly taken over by throbbing pain. I fight it the best I can and continue run until I'm safe in my room under my blanket.

I can't believe I thought Court wanted to kiss me. I am such an idiot. Why would he want to kiss me after all that I did to him? All I ever do is hurt him. I won't blame him, if he never wants to talk to me again.

"Can I come in?" Court asks knocking on my door.

"No!"

"Please."

"Fine." I bury myself deeper under the covers, so only my forehead is visible.

Court walks in and sits right next to me. I really can't face him. "Can we talk?"

"Ah huh."

"I'm sorry for what I said out there. I didn't mean it."

"You don't owe me any apologizes. I should have never kissed you. I'm really sorry." I say poking my head out from under the blanket.

"No, I'm happy you did it. I've been wanting to kiss you for awhile."

"You have?" I ask sitting to attention with my heart racing again.

—

"Emma, I wish things could've been different. I wish we were here together as a couple, and not as friends. I don't wanna feel anything for you, but I do."

"You still have feelings for me?"

"Yes, I do. Even after you tore my heart to pieces, I'm still crazy about you. You're the only person I want to be with." He looks down at his lap and says, "I wish I could've been the guy you picked."

"I wish you were the guy I picked too. I wish I could go back in time and change everything." I say without thinking. He places his warm hand on my face. I slowly turn my head, to meet it with a kiss.

"I can be the guy you pick now."

I don't say anything. I want him to be the guy I pick now. Court stares deeply into my eyes, as his breathing becomes heavier. "I'm gonna kiss you now. If you don't want me to just say stop." His lips close on mine. I search my whole body and mind for a sign to make me stop him, but there isn't one.

His lips touch mine; making every inch of me spin with desire. I pull him in closer to me, and get lost in his kisses.

* * *

4

<u>Love Interruption</u>

Laughter reverberates from the kitchen disturbing my sleep. My head feels like it's being split in two by an ax. Why the hell did I drink that much last night?

The laughter gets annoyingly louder. I knew I should have never let Angie sleep over, but I wasn't in the mood to argue with her. Besides, nothing happened between us. I tossed and turned all night long thinking and dreaming about Emma.

It sounds like they're celebrating in there. I hope my mom doesn't think Angie and me are back together again. I'm never traveling down that road again. Besides, I've decided, I don't care if Emma spent the weekend with Court. I'm sure they were there together as friends. All I know, is I need to get her back. I love her, and I know she still loves me.

"Oh good, you're awake," Angie says entering my bedroom wearing my T-shirt over her jeans.

She walks over and opens the blinds letting the disturbing sunlight in. I bury my head under the pillow, which now smells like her. I'm going to have to change my sheets. I don't want any reminders of what an idiot I was last night.

"Leave me alone!"

"You are such a grouch in the morning." Angie lies next to me and tries to snuggle up against me. I sit up and push her off. Whoa, my head really does feel horrible. I'm never drinking again.

"Fine then. Come into the kitchen, your mom is making breakfast. And we have a surprise for you."

"I'm not hungry. Besides, I don't like surprises."

"Oh come on. I promise you'll like this one," she says, trying to get close to me again. I move away from her once again, as I hear more laughter coming from the direction of the kitchen.

"Well just come and see the surprise." She gets up from my bed.

"Tell me what the hell it is."

She turns her head back and flashes a smile before she says, "You'll see." She exits my room. I have to find a way to get out of my life. She brings me nothing but trouble. I walk over to my pile of clothes and throw on a red T-shirt. At this point, I don't even care if it's clean or dirty.

I step into the kitchen with my eyes half closed. The smell of eggs and bacon makes me nauseous.

My eyes pop open when I see my surprise standing by the kitchen island. I scoop her up in my arms and twirl her around. Big mistake when you're hung over.

"Whoa! I've missed you too little brother," Mila says as I put her down.

"What are you doing here?"

"I've moved back."

"What about Dad?"

"Had a fight with the wife and he threw me out. Mom said I could stay here."

"For as long as she wants," My mom says putting her arm around Mila's very tan arms. I guess they forgot about the big fight they had the day Mila left six months ago. It doesn't matter, I'm happy she's back. I didn't realize how much I missed her until this moment.

"You're looking good," Mila says tapping me on my chest.

"Thanks. You do too. So what are you gonna do while you're here?"

"Maybe go back to school. I don't know yet. I already got a job at Jimmy's new café The Free Bird. I still can't believe he named it after a Lynyrd Skynyrd song."

"You know Jimmy, he's a die hard fan. That's great! You know, I'm working there too," I say, grabbing an apple from the counter and taking a bite.

"Yeah, I know. Jimmy already told me." Mila says raising her thin eyebrow. "So are you still interested in becoming a tattoo artist?"

"Yeah. Why?"

"Cause I talked to my friend Dan who owns Ever Inked tattoo parlor, and he said you can do an apprenticeship with him next year. He's only gonna charge you five thousand dollars. I know that's a lot, but its also less then many other tattoo artists will charge you."

I feel energy run through my veins. "That sounds great! I have more than half saved up already. I'm pumped."

"I wanna be your first victim," my mom says frying up some more bacon. I look at her in shock, as she stands in front of the stove with her blond hair tied back in a messy bun. I can't remember the last time she cooked anything.

"We'll see." I grunt. I'm still pissed at her for having a hand in ruining my relationship with Emma.

"Now, Dan does have one big rule before you start," Mila says with her crystal clear aqua blue eyes open wide.

"What?

"You have to finish high school. He won't take you, if you don't have a diploma."

"No problem." I'm not sure if that's really his rule or Mila's. She has always been keen on making sure I finish school. I think it's because she dropped out. She always said it was the biggest mistake she ever made.

"Don't worry, he's gonna finish," Angie confirms, wrapping her arms around my waist. I had almost forgotten she was still here.

"Yeah I am." I pull away from her.

Mila looks confused by my reaction to Angie. "What's going on? Are you guys arguing?"

"You know how your brother is. He hates the mushy stuff," Angie says coming to stand by me again.

"Whatever. Mila it's good to have you back. But I gotta go now." I grab my keys and head towards the door. I have to get out of this house.

"Where are you going?" My mom asks forming an attitude.

"Out!"

"Can I come?" Angie asks.

"NO!"

I walk out into the mid-morning sun. I jump in my truck, and jump right out, before the leather seat even has the chance to give me third degree burns. This sun is intense today. I jump back in, turn the ignition on, and hope the air conditioner does its magic quickly.

I turn up my radio that is playing *One Shot* by O.A.R. I still remember holding Emma at their concert. I think that was the day I realized I was feeling more than I should for her. Damn it! Why did I screw that up?

I drive for a while, thinking about Mila being back home, and what it might mean. I also think about the good lead she had for my future in tattooing. All I want to do is go tell Emma the good news.

I drive right into Cypress Oak. I pass all of the huge houses, and wonder, which one belongs to Court. I'm not sure I can compete with all of this. I knew the kid was rich, but I never thought he was this rich. Each house I pass, is bigger than the next. No wonder Emma likes him so much. What am I saying, she doesn't care about things like that. I at least hope she doesn't.

I have to talk to her. I need for her to give me a chance to explain why I kissed Angie. I wonder if she's back yet. And if she is, is she back with Court by her side?

Before I know it, I find myself parked outside of her house. I see her parent's cars in the driveway, but notice there is no life coming from her house. She's still not home. This sucks!

* * *

I open my eyes expecting to see Court lying next to me, but he's not here. I wonder when he left. Does he regret everything that happened between us last night. I'm not sure how I feel yet. I'm not sure how to process all of this. Yesterday, at this time, I was thinking about being with Nash and now I'm thinking about being with Court. So much has changed in a couple of hours.

"Emma, are you awake?" My mother asks, stepping into my room without knocking. I really can't stand when she does this.

"Yeah."

She stands in front of my bed and looks around as if she's searching for something. Could there be a possible way that she knows? I hope not. I pull the covers over my face so she can't really see me.

"Are you okay?" She asks.

"Yeah."

"Are you sure?"

"Yes."

"Well you better come down soon. We're leaving in half an hour."

"Okay, I'll be right down." I really hope she doesn't suspect anything. I'm still shocked over what happened last night. I can't believe I'm no longer a virgin. I always thought I'd feel different. Maybe I look different.

I jump out of bed. Ouch! My legs feel so sore. Sex hurts even after it's over. I can't believe I slept with Court. This is not how I thought this weekend would end.

I stand in front of the bathroom mirror and really take a good look at myself to see if there is anything different about me. Nope, still the same boring me. Same flat brown hair, same brown eyes, same pointy nose, same dull lips, and same bluish-purple mark on the right side of my neck.

Wait!

What?

Ohmigod, what the hell is this bruise on my neck? Is that a hickey? Ohmigod, Court gave me a hickey. It's huge, about the size of a quarter or maybe even a half dollar. I can't believe this.

How am I supposed to hide this? I don't even have make-up to try to cover it up. And it's way too hot to wear a turtleneck, not like I even own one. I swear I could kill Court right now.

Damn him!

I wonder what's going through his head right now. Does he regret what we did last night, and that's why he snuck out of my room in the middle of the night. Maybe I was another notch on his bedpost, just like Angie. I hope not.

I look at my neck one last time and decide to flip all of my hair forward to the right side of my neck. I hate wearing my hair like this, but I'll have to bear it, to hide the fact that last night actually happened. God, I hope this helps, until I know how to deal with it.

I finish getting ready and begin to walk slowly down the stairs. I'm so scared to face Court. I don't know what I'm supposed to say to him.

I take each step apprehensively, assuming, and uncomfortable.

Having sex was nothing like I expected. It hurt a lot. I mean a lot. That famous sex book lied. I can't imagine how any virgin could have an orgasm their first time.

I just wish I understood what I was feeling right now. I always thought I would see fireworks and be head over heels in love the moment I lost my virginity. I never thought I'd feel so lost, so incomplete.

I stand in front of the door consumed with fear. I know once I walk outside I'm going to have to face Court. What if he doesn't even acknowledge me? Or what if he now thinks we're in a relationship? Maybe, there's a bus I could take back to Cypress Oak, so I don't have to face him yet.

"Come on we have to get going," My father says, walking right past me, opening the door for me. Here goes nothing.

I step outside and immediately spot Court talking to his parents. The ocean breeze blows his chestnut hair away from his beautiful face. When I first met Court in kindergarten, I would never have thought we would become friends; much less that he would be my first.

His mother says something, which makes him smile, and causes my heart to go weak. A part of me wants to run the other direction, but the other part of me wants to run to him. It's weird how close I feel to him right now.

He looks up and stares at me. I smile, and watch his smile slowly disappear. Oh God, he does regret it. He begins to walk towards me looking down at the ground. Maybe I was bad and he's afraid to say something. I wish I knew what he was thinking.

"Hey," I say giving him my bag.

"Hey."

"Can you believe this weekend is over?"

"Ah hum."

I really hate making small talk. "Umm…I guess we need to tal…."

"Here you are," my mother says interrupting the beginning of our morning after talk. "You left this upstairs." She hands me the plastic bag containing Nash's sweatshirt. Yesterday, I wanted to burn it, now I feel guilty holding it.

"Thank you." My mother stands in front of me just looking at me. She tucks her hair behind her left ear. I guess I get that little habit from her. Her eyes gloss over like glass, and before I know it, she lunges her arms towards me, in a hug. She's squeezing me so tight, I can't even breathe. "Mom, what's wrong?"

"Nothing. I just can't believe you're going to be a junior tomorrow. My baby girl is growing up too fast." Does she know? But how? No, she doesn't know; there's no way.

"Let the girl go," my father says walking by.

My mother releases me, gives me a kiss on my check and walks away. "Okay that was weird," I say, still staring at my mother, who is now hugging Mrs. Dobberson goodbye.

"Yeah, I guess. Well, I better finish loading the car," Court replies walking past me.

"Okay." I walk over to his car confused. I knew it was going to be weird when I saw him this morning, but I really didn't believe he would be this cold towards me.

Both Mr. and Mrs. Dobberson say a quick goodbye, before getting into their BMW. The only person who does seem sad to see me go is Court's youngest brother Toby. He runs up and gives me a tight hug. I feel bad for not spending more time with him down here.

Court gets into his car before I can even walk around towards the other side. If my parents weren't in the car with us, I would tell him exactly how he's making me feel.

I find myself looking out my window, while my parents are fast asleep in the back seat. Court is driving, not even glancing my way. My head feels like a mixed salad where all the ingredients do not mesh well together.

I can't believe he is treating me this way. I glance at him and notice he also looks as exhausted as I am from thinking. He slowly turns his head, our eyes meet, and he gives me a weak smile.

"It's okay. We can forget last night. It doesn't have to mean anything," I whisper, trying to give him an easy way out, for feeling like he needs to be with me.

"What? It's not like that."

"Then what is it like? Because I'm really confused right now."

—
49

"Emma, I really think we need to talk, but not with your parents sleeping in the backseat.

"I just feel…." I hear my father shift around and realize he's right. We can't talk right now.

I turn my attention back towards the window and close my eyes. I begin to remember instances of last night that are no longer lost in a fog. I remember Court kissing me, his hands exploring me in ways he never had before. Our clothes slowly coming off as our kissing intensified. I remember him putting on a condom, and then entering my body with a sharp pain, making me gasp for air. I remember holding him tight and snuggling up to his chest when it was over. I remember closing my eyes and dreaming of—Nash.

Why does he always have to creep back into my head? I don't want to feel anything for him, but I do. Even after experiencing my first time with Court, I still can't stop thinking about Nash.

I open my eyes just as Court pulls into my driveway. My parents hop out of the car, stretch right before they grab their bags, and say their goodbyes to Court, making sure to thank him over ten million times. I just wish they would go inside already, so I can finally have "the talk" with him.

"Emma, don't be too long. Remember you need to get things ready for school tomorrow," My mother says before going inside.

"I'll be right there."

"Alright then, I'm gonna head out," Court states as soon as my parents enter the house. Is he serious? He's not going to talk to me?

"Okay."

"I'll see you later."

This is how Angie must have felt, when she realized Court was just using her for sex. I start to stomp away, but then decide, I have to say something. I turn back toward his car and blurt out, "You're a dick!"

"What?"

"You finally got me, so now you're done with me."

"What are you talking about?"

"You've slept with me, and now you're moving on. I never thought you were this type of person."

"I didn't use you for sex," Court says walking towards me.

"Oh really, then why are you acting this way? Do you regret it?"

"No. Emma what happened between us was amazing. I was so happy holding you in my arms last night."

"Then why are you acting like this?" I ask more confused than ever.

"Do you know you talk in you're sleep?"

"I do?" Oh no! What did I say?

"Yeah. There I was holding you in my arms watching you sleep, feeling happy you were back in my life again. And then you said 'I love you...Nash.' You know how I felt? I knew then, I didn't have you back."

"I'm sorry. I didn't mean to say...."

"I feel more for you than I have ever felt for anyone else, but I can't go through this again. It was too painful the first time. I'm sorry." Sadness takes over his baby blue eyes. "I really think you need to deal with your feelings for Nash." He gets into his car, and drives away leaving me befuddled.

I know he's right. I have to do something about Nash. As special as what happened between Court and me, there is still a huge part of my heart that still wants Nash. Maybe I should go see him in person, and have the talk we were supposed to have. After last night I'm not sure we can work things out, but I need to find out.

I run in my house and ask my mother if I could use her car. I make up some stuff about taking Court's phone by accident. My mother doesn't seem to care. She's too busy talking to someone on the phone. Her face looks pale and filled with worry. I hope it's nothing bad. I'm sure I will hear about it later. I have to go to Nash's right now.

I make sure to take the bag containing Nash's sweatshirt and the envelope with the portrait he drew of me. If everything goes well, these things will remain in my life, but if they don't, I'm getting rid of them along with Nash.

Gripping the steering wheel tight, I fly down route 17 with my thoughts spinning. Can Nash and me have a real relationship after what I did with Court? And what about Court? What's our relationship going to be like now? Why did I sleep with him? On the other hand, in a weird way I'm happy it was him. Court and me now really do have a special relationship. I'll talk to Nash and then take it from there.

My heart starts beating like crazy when I turn down his street. Maybe I should have called him first, I just hope he's home and his mother is not.

I park my car a few houses away from his. I can't believe I'm going to do this. I try to catch my breath, but no air wants to enter. What am I going to say to him? Should I start with "Why did you kiss Angie?" What if he rejects me? Maybe this is a huge mistake.

His front door swings open, and I hold my breath. My stomach quickly sinks so hard I swear I have bricks in it. Angie walks out with a huge smile plastered on her face. She's wearing Nash's black Billabong T-shirt. It's the same shirt he wore the night he first kissed me at the Stone Solid concert.

How many times will I have to be slapped in the face before I realize Nash is not right for me? I grab a pen out of the glove compartment box and write him a note on the envelope. As soon as I see Angie is gone, I jump out of my car and hang the plastic bag on the white garage door handle. This whole thing with Nash is really over.

5
Shadows of the Night

"So, she just showed up without warning?" Leo asks disconnecting the stage lighting wires.

"Yup. She was in my kitchen laughing with my mom like nothing ever happened between them. Hopefully the peace between them will last for a while. Either way, it's good to have Mila back."

"Speaking of people keeping the peace, have you spoken to Sam yet? I've never seen that kid so mad."

"Yeah, well his girl shouldn't have gotten into my business. If it wasn't for her, I would still have a chance with…."

"Don't say it Nash. It wasn't Britney who made you kiss Angie."

"I know. Trust me, I know," I say, picking up blue plastic cups that seem to have taken over his backyard. "I swear those people last night were all real pigs. Don't they know what a trash can is for?"

"I don't think so. Anyway, did anything else happen between Angie and you last night?"

"Hell no! I'm not making that mistake again."

"I remember not that long ago you were in love with that mistake," Leo reminds me, lifting his right eyebrow higher than his left.

"That was a long time ago. I'm in love with someone else now."

"So you say."

"What's that supposed to mean?" He's really starting to agitate me.

"I just feel like you fell in love with this girl a little too quickly. What is it about her that has you going crazy?"

Why is he asking me this? It doesn't matter; I can answer his question without even thinking about it. "She makes me feel like I can be myself around her. She's easy to talk to and doesn't judge me. But most of all, she's honest. Emma is not trying to play games with me. She's not looking for the next best thing, I'm enough for her."

"Sounds like my girlfriend Jen, and that's why I love her. Well then try to not mess it up anymore than you have," he says laughing, as he pulls out another garbage bag. He's right, I have to make everything right with Emma and never do anything to push her away again.

I pull out my phone to see if maybe she sent me a message. I pull out my phone and realize I forgot to turn it back on last night. As soon as the power brings it back to life I notice I have a voice message.

Adrenaline fills every inch of me when I hear it's from Emma. Her voice sounds so sad. I'm such an idiot for getting mad at her and sending her that stupid text. It's good to know it's not too late.

"Yo, I'm sorry, but I gotta bail. Emma wants to talk. I gotta go home and change."

"No prob. Call me later, and let me know how it goes."

I can't believe Emma still wants to talk. Things from this moment forward are going to be perfect. I will not let them fall apart again.

I look up at the sky, and for the first time, in a long time, I feel as if my brother Ben is here with me. O.A.R plays again on my radio and I sing every word loudly as I head back home.

After I change I'll drive to Emma's and wait for her to arrive. Hopefully when she sees me she'll run straight into my arms. I can't wait to hold her. I pull over right in front of my house and jump out of my truck. I haven't felt this happy, since the day Emma told me she loved me.

As I walk towards my house I notice a bag hanging on the handle of my garage door. I don't know why but I'm afraid to see what's in it. I cautiously saunter over to it, as if the bag contains a bomb or something else explosive.

The plastic rattles in my hands. I open up the bag, and my heart shatters as if a bat hit it. I pull out the manila envelope and read the note on it:

Dear Nash,

I'm returning your stuff. I don't need it or you in my life anymore.

I'm happy with Court now. I hope you're happy with Angie too.

Goodbye forever,

Emma.

I take my sweatshirt and throw it across my front yard. Why is this happening? How is it that one minute I can be so happy, and the next I could feel so destroyed? I can't cry, I won't cry.

* * *

Trying to cover up this hickey is not easy at all. I tried using some of my mother's cover-up, but all it did was make it look like an orange bluish purple mark. This sucks. I can't even wear a sweatshirt, since it's like 90 degrees outside. I guess I have to put all my hair towards the front of my neck again. I hope no one sees it.

I look in the mirror, and once again, try to see if I look any different. I feel like I really haven't dealt with the fact that I've had sex. I'm returning to Cypress Oak High School a non-virgin. Hopefully, no one knows. I don't think Court would tell anyone. At least I hope he wouldn't.

I wonder how he is going to react when he sees me at school. Is he still going to be mad? My stomach is tight with agony. I'm not sure if I'm ready to go back. I feel like I'm about to jump out of a plane without a parachute.

"Emma! Britney's outside," my father announces up the stairs.

"Okay, I'll be right there." I take one more look to make sure my hickey is well covered. Okay here goes nothing.

"Oh my God Emma, is that what you're wearing on your first day of school? I got you all those cute clothes, and that's what you've decided to wear," my mother says giving me a disapproving look.

"What's wrong with it?"

"Emma, it's a pair of old cut off jean shorts and a Ramones tank top. You have to have something better than that to wear. And your hair, at least get it off your face." I duck, moving out of the way before she can push it back, and expose my marked skin.

"I gotta go, Britney is waiting. Bye." I run out of the house before my mother can complain anymore about how I look.

"Hey," I say jumping into Britney's car.

"Hey. I'm so glad you're back" She leans over and gives me a hug. "So how was the Hamptons?"

"Good. How was everything here?" I wish I could put my hair up. This sticky heat is making it hard for me to keep it purposely on my neck.

"Good. Same old same." She gives me a sideways glance, and with her olive green eyes apprehensively says, "I'm sorry I sent you that picture. I was on my way to tell him to call you, when I caught him. I needed you to see what an asshole he is."

"No worries. He's history." The words sting my mouth as they come out.

"Good. Oh by the way, Sam became my personal hero that night."

"How?"

"Well, when Nash realized I sent you a picture, he flipped out and called me a fucken bitch."

"Are you serious?" I'm starting to realize I don't know him at all.

"Yeah, but Sam warned him never to talk to me that way again."

"AWE! That Sam, he's a keeper."

"Yes he is. So did anything happen between Court and you this weekend?" She asks driving into the first parking space she finds.

"No. Nothing at all." I want to tell her everything, but I feel like I should really deal with it first.

The parking lot is full with my classmates who are all dressed in their new school outfits excited to start a new year. They are all fools. Don't they remember how much school sucked a couple of weeks ago?

I raise my shoulders to my ears in a visceral reaction, as three girls shriek as loud as their vocal cords allow them to when they see each other. Really? They've only been apart for two months and I'm sure they texted and FaceBooked each other hundreds of times. I really can't stand my classmates.

Britney and me head straight to the bathroom as soon as we enter the red brick institute, I mean high school, to get away from the phoniness going on all around us. How am I going to deal with another school year?

"So what's up with your hair?" Britney asks fixing hers in the mirror.

"What do you mean?

"You never wear it like that."

"I'm trying a new look," I say making sure it's doing its job of hiding my ugly hickey.

"Yeah right." Before I can stop her she pushes back my hair and her eyes shoot wide open as she focuses on my neck. "Ohmigod! Who gave you the hickey?"

"Court," I whisper.

"You guys hoo…." She steps back intensely looking at me. "Ohmigod! Ohmigod! Ohmigod! Emma you had sex!" How did she figure it out? I swear, sometimes I think she's a witch. "You had sex with Court!" She gives me a big hug.

"Shh! I did, but please don't tell anyone."

"How was it?"

"Okay, I guess. It hurt a lot."

"Yeah, it's gonna hurt a couple more times, but then it will feel a lot better. So does this mean you guys are back together?"

"Not exactly," I answer, tucking my hair behind my left ear.

"What do you mean not exactly? Please don't tell me he dipped it and skipped it?"

Before I can explain, the door swings open and lets in a group of freshmen girls, who look excited and scared at the same time. They stay frozen in their place waiting to see our reaction. I smile and help them relax a little. If they only knew, I'm not the one they should fear.

"Come on," I say pulling the door open. I walk out only to run right into Court. He looks so handsome in his new plaid blue and red shirt. He gives me a small smile. Unexpectedly, his eyes shoot open when he notices my neck. Damn, I forgot to pull my hair towards my right side again.

"Did I do that?" He asks, acting like he just found out I was pregnant or something."

I quickly flip my hair forward and nod. I'm trying to look him in the eyes, but find myself feeling shy.

It finally hits me that he has actually seen me naked.

And I kind of saw him naked too.

We have seen each other naked!

I can't deal with this right now. I turn around and walk away as fast as I can. It's all rushing into my head way too fast. I slept with Court!

Court and I had sex! I had sex! I'm no longer a virgin. AAAAAAHHH!

"Will you slow down," Britney says finally stopping me.

"I-can't-breathe." I try but I really can't breathe.

"What did he do to you?" She holds me in her arms. I shake my head, take a deep breath and tell her everything. How we ended up in bed together. How he snuck out of my room. How I said Nash's name while I was sleeping. I tell her everything before first period even has a chance to start.

"Oh wow. But why did you run away from him now? He looked like he might want to talk to you."

"Because it has finally hit me what I did this weekend."

"Emma did you want to do it? I mean you weren't forced or any…."

"No! I wasn't forced. Not at all."

"But did you wanna do it?"

"I'm not sure. I just got carried away." The bell rings and brings an end to my panic attack.

"Do you wanna go somewhere and talk?"

"No we better get to class." I can't think about anymore or I will have another panic attack.

"Fine, but we will talk later. I promise you everything is going to be okay."

"I know," I say and get up to officially start my junior year.

The first day of school is always so boring. Every teacher seems to give the same speech. After a while all I hear is blah, blah, blah, blah, blah. I only have one class with Britney, which sucks. I manage most of the day to not run into Court or any of his friends, mostly because I've been hiding.

I was hoping no one would pay any attention to me, and I could go back to blending into the hallways, but no such luck. Everyone is staring at me and whispering behind my back. Everyone who did not know my relationship with Court is over, cannot hide his or her astonishment and enjoyment of the news. All this attention is draining me.

My classes are also wearing me out. I walk into my last class exhausted. I would like to kill the person who set up my schedule. How could they give me English Lit as my last class ? I'm too tired to deal with lectures about old books I have no interest in reading.

I walk deep into the classroom and take my usual seat in the last row by the window. I put my head down on the light wood desk and close my eyes. I really wish I were back at the arcade. I picture Nash leaning up against a video game with his famous crooked smile. I might need rehab to get him out of my system.

Without warning, I hear a shriek and I feel every hair on the back of my neck rise. I recognize that voice from anywhere. Christy LaVandel! Oh God, why does she have to be in this class.

I look up just in time to see her loop her arm into Court's. He's laughing at whatever she whispers in his ears. She looks at him with her big royal blue eyes, making me sick. Christy slowly turns her head and notices me. Her stupid smile becomes wider exposing all her white teeth.

"Come on Court, lets go sit over there!" She makes sure to say it extra loud. She grabs his hand to lead him, but he doesn't move. Instead, he finally realizes I'm also in this class.

His smile slowly disappears and his eyes seem to fill with pity. I quickly bring my eyes down to my desk. My insides burn with rage. Why did he look at me that way? Does he feel sorry for me? I don't need his pity. In fact, I don't need him. So we slept together, big deal. It was a mistake. Unfortunately, a mistake I can't ever take back.

I try my best not to look his way. How am I going to survive a whole year like this? And just when I think it can't get any worse, Mrs. Kennel announces, "I will be putting you in reading groups of four. You will be in these groups for the whole year. You will be asked to read one book a month and use your reader's notebook to answer questions. At the end of each semester, you will have to do a group presentation that will be worth 30 percent of your grade."

Oh God, not another project. Please don't let me be grouped with either Court or Christie. My stomach twists and turns as she calls out the groups. Following the second group Mrs. Kennel announces, "The next group is Emma Paige, Lilly Powers." Only two more names to go, please let it be two that I don't know. "Christy LaVandel." NO! Why? "And Court Dobberson." Is she kidding me? My school year is off to a bad start. Hello God, did you not hear my prayers?

Court turns back and gives me a small grin. I don't smile back. Things can't get any worse. The bell finally rings giving me a chance to escape.

I grab my bag and run out of the class before Court even has a chance to get out of his seat. This is going to be a tough school year. Maybe I can convince my mother to home school me.

I walk into my house trying to shake off the day. So much has happened in these last few weeks, I am mentally exhausted.

"Emma is that you?" My mother calls out from her office. I can't believe she's home.

"Yeah. I thought you were teaching a class today?"

"I am. It's an online class," she says coming into the kitchen. "I wanted to talk to you about something, and I was hoping we could do it now."

"Mom, can it wait? I'm really tired and I jus...."

"Actually it can't. I need to talk to you before your father comes home."

"Okay. What's up?"

"Lets go sit at the table." She's making me nervous now. I hope there's nothing going on between my father and her. We both sit at our round maple wood kitchen table. The sun is coming in through the window, illuminating half the table. She takes a deep breath, and tucks her hair behind her left ear. "I'm going to ask you a question, and I want you to be honest with me. I promise, I will not get mad. I'm your mother, and I love you no matter what."

"What is it? You're really scaring me now."

"Are you and Court having sex?"

"What?" Ohmigod, she knows. But how? Maybe I do look different. But why didn't I see it.

"The other night, I saw Court sneaking out of your room at three in the morning. He was putting his shirt back on."

"A…a…."

"Was this your first time?" She asks squeezing her fingers tensely with her other hand. This information seems to have aged her twenty years.

I nod. I can't believe we are having this conversation.

"How was it?"

"Mom?!'

"No, no! I didn't mean it like that. I mean, how are you feeling?"

"I don't know." I can't tell her, I feel embarrassed. Embarrassed that I slept with Court without really knowing if it was what I really wanted to do, or if it was out of anger from feeling betrayed by Nash. All I do know is, it was a big mistake.

My mother's brown eyes fill with tears, waiting for her to blink so they can make their way out. "Were you careful? I mean did you use something?"

I try to speak, but my voice gives out, and I only make a squeak, as I nod my head.

"Good."

We sit in an uncomfortable silence. I stare out the window at the cars parked outside; there's no way I can look at her right now. In fact, I'm not sure I will ever be able to look her in the eyes again. Why does every other teenager get to lose their virginity without their parents finding out?

"Are you mad at me?" I whisper, putting my head down on my folded arms. I can't even imagine what my punishment is going to be.

"No. I mean I wish you had waited until you were older, like in your thirties and were married for a couple years. But that's just the mom side of me, who wants you to stay my little girl forever." All of a sudden, I realize why she almost started to cry the morning we were leaving the Hamptons.

"The side of me that remembers what it was like to be your age, and sexually active knows I should be here for you." Did my mother just say she was having sex at my age? But I thought she was a big geek, who didn't have a boyfriend until college where she met my father.

"I wish I would have had someone to talk to. Especially the way I experienced my first time." Oh God, I do not want to hear about my mother's first time. Ill, I think I'm starting to picture it. Ill! Think of baseball. Wait, that's for guys who…oh forget it. "I want to be here for you in the way I needed my mother there for me." She places her hand over my arm and says, "Do you have any questions? Or, is there something you would like to talk about?"

"Does Dad know?" *Please don't let him know.*

"No." *Whew!*

"Are you gonna tell him?"

"Only if you want me to."

"No!" It's bad enough she knows, I don't need him finding out too.

"I did make you an appointment with Dr. Harper."

"What? Why? Wait, who's Dr. Harper?" Is she sending me to a shrink?

"She's my gynecologist. I want her to discuss with you all of your options for birth control. To be honest, I would love for you never to have sex again, but I know that's not going to happen. Especially now that you're back together with Court."

Oh no, she thinks we are back together. I can't tell her the truth. I don't want her to know my first time was a one-night stand. She will lose all respect for me. "Okay." I smile, but all I really want to do is cry. "Can I go to my room now?"

My mother tries to smile as her face falls. "Yes."

I get up, but I don't run upstairs. Instead, I walk over to her and give her a tight hug. "Thank you for this."

"I love you honey. And I don't care how old you get or what happens in your life, you will always be my little girl."

I hug her tighter and finally release tears I've been holding back. I really wish I were still her little girl, who didn't care about anything but spending time with my parents and playing with my toys again.

6
Can't Stop

For the last week I've been pacing the hallways of Monticello High School like an empty vessel. I really miss my brother Ben. He would know exactly what to say to make me feel normal again. He would probably have kicked my ass for what I did to the girl I love.

He would also kick my ass for being a bad friend to Sam. Ever since our little confrontation at Leo's party, we haven't said one word to each other. I hate to admit it, but I miss the kid.

The truth is he's not the one I'm mad at. I'm not even mad at Britney for being a meddling idiot. I'm mad at myself for messing up time after time. Anyway, Sam thinks I'm still angry with him, and I know he won't approach me, until I show him we're cool.

I walk out into the parking lot right after my last class. I spot him sitting on the hood of his car reading a book. "How many more months 'til we graduate?"

He looks up and grins, "I know, right?"

"So, you'll never guess who's back at my house."

"Who?"

"Mila."

67

"No way! Really? How is she?"

"Good so far. I mean she and my mom are acting like they're best friends. I just hope it lasts."

"I know. Hey, do you have to work tonight?" He asks jumping down from his hood.

"Nah. Why?"

"There's a party at Gore Lake, do you wanna go?"

"Whose party is it?"

"Cypress Oak, it's their back to school party. Britney says they do it every year."

I don't think I'm ready to see Britney. But wait, if Britney is going, I'm sure Emma will be there too. "Yo, you think I can bring Leo?"

"I don't see why not?"

"Sounds like a plan."

As I start to drive home, I come to the realization that Emma will probably be at the party with Court. I'm not sure if I can see them together. There's no way I can sit there and watch them hold hands, or even worse, kiss. Maybe I shouldn't go. I walk into my house feeling deflated.

"Hey, you're home early," Mila says sitting on the couch watching some stupid reality show.

"Yup." I walk straight into my room, and lay on my bed, with no energy to even open up my blinds, and let the sun into the darkness that has become my world.

"Okay, I'm over you're moodiness," Mila says entering my room. I swear the women in this house do not know how to knock on a door. "What's going on with you? Are you fighting with Angie again?"

"This is not about Angie, it's about Emma."

"Who's Emma?" She asks sitting at the foot of my bed. She pushes her long hair back as her eyes illuminate. "Wait, is she the girl from the drawing you did?"

"How do you know about that picture?"

"I found it when I was looking for a shirt."

I want to be mad at her for going through my stuff, but I can't be. "Yeah, that's her."

"So what happened between you and this girl Emma?"

I sit up and begin to tell her everything. I tell her about how we met, about me coming up with that stupid plan to use her to get back at Court. I tell her about how I fell in love with her, and how I broke her heart. And I tell her about how I've lost her for good.

"Wow. Little brother you really messed up," she states shaking her head.

"You think I don't know that?"

"Okay. So how do you plan to get her back?"

"Did you not hear me? She's with Court now. I've lost her for good."

"No. It's just become a challenge. If you really love her, the way you say you do, you'll have to fight for her. Besides, you've taken her away from Court once before, I'm sure you can do it again."

She's right. I can't just sit back and let the girl I'm in love with fall in love with another guy. "What are you doing tonight?" I ask her, feeling confident once again.

"Nothing. Why?"

"You wanna go to a party?" I'm getting Emma back.

* * *

69

My first gynecologist appointment was horrible. It's the most embarrassing thing I've ever been through. I had to put my legs up on metal stirrups, as she inspected my most delicate of organs, all the while my stomach cramped in pain. I felt humiliated.

After my check up, Dr. Harper went over all the different forms of birth control. She talked about, pills, rings, IUDs, and shots, so much it made me dizzy. My mother sat next to me trying to act like she was cool with everything, but I know deep down inside, she was freaking out. God knows, I was.

I decided on the pill for my non-existing sex life. I know I won't be having sex for a super long time. Maybe I'll honor my mother's wish and won't have sex until I'm thirty.

After my appointment, my mother and I decided to get some ice cream. "So what are you doing tonight? I thought we have a girl's night and…."

"Oh Mom, I was hoping to go to the school lake party. I'm not grounded or anything. Right?"

"No. You're not grounded. Is Court going to take you?" She asks taking a spoonful of her vanilla ice cream. I can never understand why, with so many amazing flavors out there, anybody can just eat plain vanilla.

"No. I was hoping you'd let me use your car."

"Why isn't he picking you up? Are you guys okay? You know sometimes sex changes a…."

"No! Everything is fine. He's just meeting me there. He has a football game, and he'll head to the party right after." I don't know how much longer I can pretend I'm dating Court. Especially since he and I haven't spoken one word to each other in almost a week.

In school, I do my best to avoid him. I enter my English class, right when the bell rings, and try my best to be the first one out the door. I've also been lucky Mrs. Kennel has not made us meet with our reading groups yet.

"Okay, but be careful," she states worriedly giving me a look of nervousness.

"I will."

I run upstairs to get ready when we get home. I really need to have fun tonight. I'm tired of feeling sad. I look at my neck and am happy my hickey is almost gone. It's only a light brownish yellow mark right now, which has been easy to cover with make-up. I'm so happy no one ever discovered it.

I put on my favorite worn-in jeans and my light blue sweatshirt. I really think the best part about being alone is not caring one bit about what I'm going to wear. Of course my mother hates my outfit, but she wouldn't be my mother if she didn't.

I head straight to Britney's house to pick her up. My heart almost leaps out of my chest when I see whom she's walking with down her stairs. It's her brother Johnny. He moved further upstate last year for college and decided to stay there for the summer. I haven't seen him since Christmas.

He looks even better. His caramel colored hair has grown some since the last time I saw him. He walks over to my side of the car, looks at me with his cool vivid green eyes that have the perfect blue undertone in them, and grins, making my heart melt a little. I can't help it.

Johnny has always had this affect on me. When I was a kid, I lived and breathed for him. I wish I could say he felt the same way, but he didn't. To him, I was like another kid-sister he had to put up with.

He opens my door and pulls me out. I wrap my arms around him and squeeze him as hard as he's squeezing me. "How are you?" Yes, he still makes my heart flutter. Oh God, he smells so good.

"Good. What are you doing here?"

"I came down for the weekend, 'cause I missed my little sister, and had to come back to see her," Johnny says putting his arm around Britney's shoulders. I've always been jealous of the great relationship they have. I remember always leaving their house, wishing I had a brother like him.

"Yeah right. He's here to borrow some money from my mom. He knows she's a sucker when it comes to him," Britney announces.

"Thanks for throwing me under the bus. Oh well, what am I gonna do?"

"Like mom said get a job!" She says making air quotes.

"I don't remember you being this annoying," Johnny says wrinkling his nose the same way Britney does, when she doesn't agree with something.

"Well I'm glad you're back." I lean against my car.

"Thank you. I'm actually glad I'm back too. So where are you ladies heading to tonight?"

"To the back to school party at Lake Gore. You wanna come?" I ask, hoping he says yes. I really need someone to hang out with, in case Britney decides to spend all her time with Sam.

"A high school party? I don't think so."

"Oh come on. You can keep me company while Britney hangs out with Sam," I say.

"Okay. Besides, I'd like to meet this Sam and make sure he's good enough for my little sister," Johnny says, nudging his hip against Britney.

"Don't you mess with him," Britney warns, tugging Johnny's hair. We both start to laugh.

We all get into my car, and head out to have some fun. It's so great to have Johnny back home, even if it's only for the weekend.

We arrive just as the sunset descends into fiery streaks across the sky, and allows the ascending light of the moon to shine on us now. The Lake is packed with students from Cypress Oak High School, and some other people from the surrounding schools that were invited.

Every year the town of Cypress Oak allows us to have a back to school party at Lake Gore. It's been happening since my mother was a teenager. I first came when I was a freshman, but skipped it last year because I was with Jason and he hated this scene. It's weird to be back here, in a weird way it really makes me miss him.

It's funny how even at a Lake party we are separated into our high school caste system. The beautiful people have taken over an area of the beach by the fire pits. While my group of friends have taken over the picnic tables by the woods. All the other groups scatter in-between. Music blasts throughout the whole lake area, thanks to the DJ, I'm sure was hired by a parent of one of the rich kids. I wish they would play something that's not constantly playing on the radio.

Everyone is as happy as I am to see Johnny, especially all the girls. They each make it a point to give him a hug and kiss. I can tell he loves all this attention. He had the same kind of attention in high school. I swear, he had a new girlfriend each week.

73

Minutes after we arrive, Sam appears. I'm happy to see he's alone. I was a little nervous Nash would be with him. I don't think I could deal with it, if he had shown up.

"So you're my little sister's boyfriend," Johnny says, trying his best to look tough.

I can tell Sam is nervous meeting him. Knowing Johnny, he's going to use this to mess with him. "Um, yeah. Nice to meet yah."

"Yeah, whatever. You'd better not be sleeping with my sister, or I'm gonna have to kill yah," Johnny says stepping up to Sam, who's color has vanished from his face. I burst into laughter, almost spitting out my Coke. I know Johnny wouldn't even hurt a fly.

"Wh-wh...I'm...."

"Leave him alone, Johnny," Britney says, rushing to Sam's rescue. "He's just fucking with you. Don't listen to him." Johnny starts to laugh, restoring Sam's missing color.

"Sorry. But I'm serious when I say this, you break her heart, I break your face, your arms, your legs, and any other body part I can think of."

"I said leave him alone!" Britney punches her brother in the stomach. They can be a very violent family at times.

"Ouch! Okaaayyy. Sam knows I'm just playing. Right Sam?"

"Yeah." Sam looks unsure of the correct answer.

"Whatever! Come on Sam let's go for a walk," Britney says, taking Sam by the hand and leading him away.

"You're mean," I tease Johnny.

"I know. How about we take a walk too and you tell me all about what I've missed?"

"Okay." Last year, I would've had a stroke if Johnny asked me to go for a walk. I remember Jason used to get jealous every time Johnny was around because he knew Johnny had some kind of mind control over me.

"So is this Sam good guy? Or, should I worry?"

"No, he's a good guy. A very good guy."

"Good, 'cause I've never seen Britney this hung up over a guy before," he says while we walk on the grass along the beach area.

"She's in love."

"How about you Miss Paige? Are you in love with anyone?"

I wish I could say no. Even after everything that has happened, my foolish heart still wants Nash. "It's complicated."

"Yeah, that's what I figured."

I place my hand on his arm and stop him from walking any further. "What has Britney told you?"

He turns to face me. "Just that you've been through a tough time with some loser."

"You can say that." I smile, but it rapidly disappears when I catch sight of Court standing with Christy enveloped under his arm, by the flickering flame. I hate seeing them together. It makes my stomach turn.

"Are you okay?" Johnny asks, waving his hand in front of my face for my attention.

"Yeah, I just thought I saw a friend. I guess I was wrong."

We turn around continuing our walk only to have my legs give out from under me once again. I take small breaths, trying my best to calm every organ in my body that are now shaking hysterically.

Walking straight towards us is Nash with some girl I've never seen before. I haven't seen him since that day in the rain when he told me he loved me. Now here he is with some girl I don't know.

He looks so good with his wavy hair falling down just past his chin. His golden green eyes send waves of thrill and pain from the top of my head to the tip of my toes. He unlocks his eyes from me to glance over at Court who is standing with Christy.

Ohmigod, I almost forgot I told him I was back with Court. Great, now he's going to realize Court's moved on too. Damn it. I wish I had the guts to grab Johnny's hand. I'm not ready for this. Maybe I should turn around and run.

7

Disarray

I can't believe she is standing only a few feet away from me. I didn't think I was going to find her so quickly. I wonder if Mila can hear my heart pounding like a jackhammer. She takes my hand and gives it a tight squeeze. I'm so happy she came along with me. I don't think I could do this without her.

Emma's amber brown eyes glisten as she tucks her hair behind her left ear. She is so beautiful. I have to fight the urge not to run over to her and take her in my arms.

I take my eyes off her for a second, to ascertain who is the guy standing way too close to her. I've never seen him before. Why is he with her? Where's Court?

I look over towards the beach area, where his people are all hanging out like sheep around the fire pit. I immediately spot him next to some blond girl, who is hanging all over him. What's going on? Did Emma and he break up already? I hope so. This might end up being a great night after all. Now, I need to find out who this idiot is with her.

We take a couple more steps towards her. My heart is heavy now, trying to burst right out of my chest. I really hope she doesn't run away again. I don't think I could handle again.

I reach her side and find it hard to murmur a sound. Her eyes open wide with anticipation. Whatever comes out of my mouth next, will hopefully be enough to make her want to talk to me. "Hey," I finally mange to utter. *Really? I'm so stupid.*

"Hey." Emma peels her eyes off me, and gazes over at my sister with the same look I want to give the guy she's with. This is a good sign, she's jealous. I can't help but smile.

"You must be Emma! I'm Mila. Nash's older, more beautiful, wiser sister," Mila says, when she also notices the way Emma is staring at her.

Emma's body seems to relax a little as a beautiful smile forms on her face, God she's so cute. Why can't things be different? "Oh yeah, Mila came back home." I swear, I sound like an idiot.

"It's nice to meet you."

"You too. So who's this?" Mila asks lowering her head, to look at Emma, and pointing to the asshole next to her.

"I'm Johnny." Why is he smiling like that?

"He's Johnny. Britney's older brother." Oh good, he's just her friend. I think.

"Britney? Britney? Oh! Sam's girlfriend! Well, it's good to meet you Britney's older brother."

"You too, Nash's older, more beautiful, and wiser sister." Mila laughs playfully tossing back her dark brown hair. "What do you say you and I go over to the picnic tables to talk about why we're at a high school party at our age. Wait, how old are you?"

"Nineteen."

"Ooouuu, a younger guy. Perfect."

"How old are you?" Johnny asks in an inquisitively wide grin. I'm still not sure if I like this guy.

"Twenty-one."

"Ooouuu, an older woman. I really like that."

Mila walks off to stand by an abandoned picnic table. She turns and beckons Johnny to join.

"I'll be right back. Will you be okay?" Johnny asks Emma.

"Yeah, I'm fine." He walks off in Mila's direction. I owe her big time.

Okay, here goes nothing. I have to make sure to tell her everything that is in my heart. "How are you?" Why can't I think of something wittier to say?

A strong gust of wind makes her hair dance around her face making my heart skip a beat. "Good," She says with an even bigger smile. I'm not sure if this is a good thing or not.

"You think we can talk?"

"We are talking." Her smile disappears and anger consumes her voice. This is not going to be easy.

"There's just a lot I need to explain," She turns her head towards where Court is standing, who now is staring at us with hatred in his eyes. Why is she looking at him? Okay, no more small talk, I need to say everything now, or I'm going to lose her. "Look Emma, I know I messed up but you gotta know I lo...."

"It's over. You don't need to say anything. Now, if you don't mind, I have to head back to my boyfriend." The word "boyfriend" stabs me right in the heart wounding me deeply.

She runs over to Court, who is no longer staring at us, but instead talking to some look-alike friend. As soon as she reaches his side, she whispers something in his ear and laughs. She's probably telling him what an idiot I am.

Court takes her in his arms and begins to kiss her. How I would love to go over there and knock him out. She's supposed to be with me, not him. Damn, I hate him!

"Hey, is everything okay?" Mila asks, coming back to stand by my side.

"No."

* * *

"I'll be right back. Will you be okay?" Johnny asks me. I want to scream NO! Please don't leave my side. I'll find you another cute girl you can talk to later, but please don't leave me alone with Nash. I don't think my heart is strong enough to deal with him yet.

Instead, I give him a gritty smile and say, "Yeah, I'm fine."

Nash looks at me with his golden green eyes have been making my heart go crazy since I've seen him. "How are you?"

"Good." I try my best to give him a huge smile. I hope he can't see how much I'm hurting.

"You think we can talk?"

"We are talking."

He takes a deep breath, "There's just a lot I need to explain." I can't listen to what he has to say right now. I look over at Court and see him staring at us with a painful expression. I also notice Christy is now gone. "Look Emma, I know I messed up but you gotta know I lo…."

I stop him short, preventing him from saying anything that will make it harder to get over him. "It's over. You don't need to say anything. Now if you don't mind I have to head back to my boyfriend."

I need to get away from him. I turn around and walk towards Court. Please don't let him reject me in front of Nash. I stand next to him and wrap my arms around his waist, taking him by surprise. His baby blue eyes look confused.

I stand on my tippy toes and whisper in his ear, "I'm sorry. But I told Nash you and I are back together, so he'll leave me alone." I plant my feet back on the ground and laugh like a stupid girl. I hope Nash is buying all of this.

Court turns to me and just when I think he's going to blow me off, he grabs me into his warm arms and kisses me. His lips make my whole body go limp. "Sorry. He was looking and I wanted it to look real." Court smiles. I can't believe how much I've missed his smile. I can't help but smile back.

"You think we can talk?" I ask hoping he'll agree.

"Yeah, come on." He takes my hand and leads me through his friends, who can't help hide their abhorrence of seeing me with him. Right before we step off the beach area, we run into Christy, who is coming out of the bathroom with her followers, I mean friends. She stops to a halt when she notices us. Her eyes spit fireballs my way. I turn around and smile, as we walk right past her. I'm sorry, I get a kick out of seeing her mad.

We sit in Court's Mercedes both trying to figure out what to say. The cold leather seat feels hard and unwelcoming. I stare out the window at everyone having a good time. I'm trying to figure out what to say as I try not to think about us having sex a couple of days ago.

I finally break the awkward silence and utter, "I'm sorry I've been weird lately. I don't know how to act around you after everything that's happened between us."

"I know what you mean. I'm sorry too. I over-reacted over you saying that idiots name while you were sleeping."

"I want us to go back to being friends again." The truth is, I want to talk about everything that has happened between us, but right now, all I can focus on, is having him back in my life.

"I agree. Wait, I thought you wanted me to be your boyfriend?" He laughs.

"I'm sorry. I just needed him to believe we were together, and realize I'm over him. Look, if you want, I'll go tell him…."

"No. This could be fun. I like the thought of being your pretend boyfriend. Especially, if I get to mess with that asshole's head. Come on lets go show off our new relationship," Court says getting out of the car. I didn't want to do this to mess with Nash's head; I lied to get him out of my life. This might be a big mistake.

We both walk towards the picnic tables holding hands. It reminds me of earlier days when we dated. Sometimes, I really miss those days.

"You ready?" Court whispers, as we get closer to my friends.

I nod. From afar, I can see Nash sitting on a table with Leo. I'm not sure I can do this.

It doesn't take long for everyone to turn their heads towards us. "What's going on?" Britney asks running over to join us.

"We're back together," Court announces to everyone over the roar of the loud booming music.

I smile and nod. I think I've lost my ability to talk.

"Ohmigod! I'm so happy for you guys!" Britney cheers, giving us big hugs. I look past her and see Nash staring at us with disgust. Regret fills every cell in my body. "You guys belong together."

"Emma!" I hear someone yell. I turn around and see Roxy.

It's only been a couple of days since I've last seen her, but it feels like it's been months. "Roxy!" I run over and give her a huge hug. "What are you doing here?"

"Got the night off from motherhood and I thought I'd come by. So I'm guessing the Hamptons were good?" she says noticing Court standing by me.

Court places his arm over my shoulders and says, "You have no idea how good." He gives me a wink, and I know exactly what's he's talking about. I shake my head laughing.

"I'm so happy for you guys. I always told Emma you were perfect for her."

"I agree one hundred percent," Court declares, giving me a kiss on the cheek. He's enjoying all of this a little too much.

I quickly glance over to see what Nash is doing and feel sadness come over me when I realize he's gone. I shouldn't have pretended to have this relationship with Court. It's not fair to Nash or Court.

No! What am saying? I have to remember about all the times he made me feel like a fool. I have to remember how I felt when I found out he was dating Angie and me at the same time. I have to remember how I felt, when I saw that picture of them kissing. My life is so much better without Nash. Or at least it will be.

8
Face Down

The fire in my stomach grows as Court puts his arm around Emma's shoulders. He lifts his head up to look at me with a smirk on his ugly ass face. He's enjoying every minute of this. I don't get why she's back with him. He's not right for her. Besides, I know deep down she's still in love with me. She has to be.

"You cool?" Leo asks jumping off the table.

"Not really."

"You wanna get out of here?"

"Yeah. Lets go find Mila." I hop off the table onto the moist dark grass. I'm done with this visual torture.

I take a couple of steps towards the other side of the picnic area, but stop when I spot Angie walking towards us with a wicked smile. This can't be good. I walk over with Leo to meet her halfway. I hope Emma hasn't laid eyes on her yet.

"Hey babe," she says trying to give me a kiss. I move away just in time. I'm getting good at dodging her lips.

"What are you doing here?"

"I came to find you, and maybe party a little." She smirks.

"How'd you find out I was here?"

"Your mom. She told me when I called. Oh come on, don't be mad." My mom can never keep her mouth shut. I knew we shouldn't have told her where we were going.

Angie's smile vanishes when she notices Emma. "I should have known that stupid bitch would be here." She tilts her head and purses her lips.

I try my best to sound as nice as I can. "Go home. I'm heading out anyway."

"Oh my God, is she back with the Golden Boy?" She starts to walk towards them.

"Where are you going?"

"I'm just gonna say hi." I know I should stop her, but this might be fun to watch. Leo and me follow her back to where everyone is standing.

"Well look who's back together again," she announces getting their attention. "Hi Court?"

"What do you want Angie?" Court asks. Emma's body stiffens as her eyes focus on me. Her amber brown eyes seem to have turned black with displeasure. I don't think this is a good idea anymore.

"I came over to say hi. And congratulate the happy couple." Her sinister smile widens, as her whole demeanor changes. She lowers her head, pointing to each of them and says, "So Emma, I'm gonna guess you haven't slept with Court yet, since he's still with you."

"Shut up." Court's voice rises, which makes me impulsively step closer to them. I will not allow him to get loud with her.

"Because you know that's how he is. He makes you feel all special and shit. And then he nails you and walks away faster than you can put your panties back on."

"I said shut up!" Court yells.

—

85

"Yo! You need to watch the way you talk to her, or you'll be dealing with me. And trust me, I wouldn't mind giving you another black eye," I spit out, jumping in between him and Angie.

"We could go for round two right now. I've been dying to kick your ass anyway," Court states stepping closer to me.

My hand immediately forms a tight fist. It will be my pleasure to hit him again.

"Stop!" Emma yells. "I'm done watching the two of you fight. Nash good luck with your girlfriend Angie, you're gonna need it." She grabs Court's hand. "Come on lets go." They walk off leaving my blood boiling.

"She's not my girlfriend!" I call out, but Emma continues to walk towards the parking lot without looking back.

"Thanks." Angie says coming to put her arms around my neck.

"I didn't do it for you. When are you gonna realize we're through."

"Why, because of that stupid girl? She doesn't want you anymore. Can't you see that? But I do."

"But I don't want you."

"Since when?"

"Since you decided to sleep with Court. Since you destroyed my relationship with Emma. I'm done with you. Leave me the hell alone." I storm off before I can hurt her any further. I have no idea what to do.

* * *

"Are you okay?" Court asks as we walk back to my car.

"Yeah," I answer, but I'm not.

"I'm really sorry about the whole thing with Angie. I deserve her anger but you don't"

"Neither of us do."

"I guess I still feel guilty about what I did to her last year. I don't even know who that guy was. I was scared you thought I was doing the same thing to you."

"Maybe for a minute or two, but then you told me why you were acting so strange, and I knew you hadn't used me. You should talk to Angie. Tell how you feel about the whole thing. It might help both of you get closure."

"You might be right. But not yet. I think I should let some time pass." A sly smile comes across his face. "Anyway, I had a lot of fun pretending to be your boyfriend."

"Me too. Thanks for everything."

"Anytime." He smiles making me feel like I'm walking on air. He still has a strong effect on me.

"There you are," Johnny says, interrupting us.

"Where's Britney?"

"She's gonna get a ride from Sam. Are you okay?" He asks looking at Court suspiciously.

"Yeah. Oh Johnny, you remember Court from school?"

"Oh yeah." Court looks at Johnny with bewilderment in his eyes. I forget Court runs with a different group, who can care less who we are.

"Johnny is Britney's brother."

"Oh yeah. How are you?"

Johnny just nods narrowing his eyes. I know he's trying to scare Court the same way he did with Sam.

"Well, I'll better get going. I'll call you tomorrow."

"Okay." Court leans in and gives me a sweet kiss on my cheek. Now that Court is back in my life, I'm not losing him again.

"So you and the...."

"Don't say it Johnny. Court is different from his friends."

"Yeah, I can tell." He sarcastically says. "Just be careful with your heart Emma Paige. You can't force it to love someone you don't."

"I'm not trying to make it love anyone right now. I think my heart and mind need a break from romance for awhile."

"I hope so."

"So what happened between Mila and you? Where did you guys disappear to?"

"Just walked around. She's a cool girl. I'm coming down next weekend to go to see Bayside in concert with her," Johnny proudly announces.

"At Cake?"

"Yup."

"But how? Britney and me have tried to get tickets, but they were sold out. How did you get tickets?" Bayside is this punk rock band Britney and me have been obsessed with since we heard the song *Masterpiece*. We were so excited when we learned they were going to be performing at the local club Cake. We tried everything we could to get tickets, but failed miserably.

"I didn't. Mila did."

"I swear Johnny you have the best luck." I wonder if Nash is going too. He'll probably take Angie. This night officially sucks. I just want to jump into my bed and try to remove the image of Nash from my head and heart.

———

I walk into my house drained from the roller coaster ride of emotions I'm feeling. I don't feel like I went to a party. It felt more like an intervention with everyone that's been a part of my life. Can't I just have a normal Friday night without any drama?

"WELL, THIS IS NOT ONLY YOUR LIFE YOU'RE MESSING WITH!" I hear my father's booming voice, from the kitchen. A knot of fear appears in my stomach, as I slowly walk into the kitchen to find out what's going on. I've never heard my father use that tone of voice, even when I ruined his favorite Journey T-shirt with hair dye.

I walk in to find my mother sitting at the kitchen table, with her hands cradling her face, while my father stands against the sink with his arms folded across his chest. His face is red with anger, as the vein on his neck looks like it's about to explode.

"Is everything okay?" I ask surprising them.

My mother lifts her head, and quickly raises her hand to her face to wipe away tears that are still falling from her face. "Yeah, yeah. Your dad and I were just talking."

"It didn't sound like you were just talking."

"It's grown up stuff." Is she serious? I'm old enough to be put on the pill, but not old enough to know what they're fighting over.

"I'm going to bed," my father says walking past me. "I'm glad you're home Emma.

"Goodnight." I look over at my mother, who has a fake smile spread across her face. "Did he find out about what I...."

"No, no. Sweetie it's really nothing. So how was the party?"

I walk over and sit in the chair right next to her. I want to tell her everything that happened tonight, but I can't. I'll only tell her bits and pieces, I know she wants to hear, but then I'm not able to hold it in anymore. I say, "Nash was there."

"What? What was he doing there?"

"I don't know."

"Did he say anything to you?"

I shake my head while trying to hold my tears back. There's a huge part of my heart that wishes I did hear what he had to say. I hate this need to want to be with him.

"Good. You don't need a boy like that in your life. I'm really happy you're back together with Court. He never made you cry, like that boy did."

"Why were you and Dad arguing?" I ask trying to change the subject. I'm tired of thinking about Nash, and I hope she'll tell me this time.

"I told you it was nothing."

"It looked like it was something."

"Emma, please! I don't want to talk about it. Tell me more about the party."

"I told you everything there is to tell."

"Oh."

"I'm actually really tired. I'm gonna go to bed." I pull my chair away from the table, realizing I really am worn out. "Goodnight mom."

She also stands up, and without warning, gives me a tight hug. "I love you, and I'm so proud to be your mother." Her voice cracks as the last words come out her mouth.

She's starting to scare me now. "I love you too Mom. Are you sure you're okay?"

She backs up and wipes her eyes again. Why do I keep making her tear up? "No, I am. It's just that, you're not my baby anymore. And every time I realize it, I get a little emotional."

"Okay." Why isn't she being honest with me? Something strange is going on, and it's terrifying me.

9
Devotion and Desire

Seeing Emma the other night made my need to have her back in my life even stronger. She's all I think about. Without her in my life, I don't feel like myself. It's horrible to feel like a part of you is missing all the time.

There has to be something I could do to get her back. If only I knew what I did to win her over the first time around. I look up at my pale ceiling wishing I had some kind of answer.

"Hey little brother," Mila says coming into my room with a bowl of cereal.

"Don't you know how to knock?" I'm really not in the mood to talk to anyone.

"Sorry."

I sit up shaking my head. "No. I'm the one who's sorry. What's up?"

"Nothing. Why are you just laying in here?"

"Not in the mood to do anything else," I reply.

"So, I really liked Emma. I can see why you like her so much."

"You only got to talk to her for a few seconds."

"I know." She sits at the end of my bed, scraping up the remaining cereal in the bowl. "But I can read people, and she seems like good people. Anyway, do you have any plans on how you're going to get her back?"

"I have no idea what to do. I know I need to talk to her, but she won't give me the time of day, which makes it hard. And now she's back with that stupid idiot. This all sucks."

"That's why I've tried my best not to fall in love." She puts her bowl down on the floor, and stretches her arms above her head only to bring them down quickly to slap my leg hard. "Oh by the way, I have a surprise for you!"

"What?"

"Bayside is gonna be playing at Cake this Friday."

"Yeah I know, but they're sold out. I've already tried to get tickets."

"Yes, but you don't have the connections I do." She winks. "I was able to get everyone tickets. I just delivered two to Leo, five to Sam, and I have two for us."

"How did you get so many tickets?"

"I said I have good connections."

"You're too much. Wait a minute, why five to Sam?"

"One for him, one for his girlfriend, one for her brother Johnny, who I'm actually digging, and two for Emma."

"But all Emma is gonna do is bring Court." Why would she get a ticket for him? I don't see this being a good thing.

"Well I told Sam not to tell them until Friday. I don't want her to say no just because Court didn't get a ticket. Hopefully Court will have other plans. Anyway, who knows if they're really dating."

"What do you mean if they're really dating? I saw them together."

—

93

"Yeah, well after talking to Johnny, I got the picture Emma was single, but this way we can really find out. If anything, we'll find a way for you to talk to her that night."

"Mila, I have no idea how you managed to get all these tickets, but I do know that you're the best sister any guy can have." I lean forward and give her a warm hug.

"I know." She smiles. "Meanwhile, is there anything you can send her to remind her of you? Maybe a picture of the two of you, or maybe you can draw her something that will remind her of the small special moments you spent together."

"I know exactly what to draw for her." I look past Mila into my open closet and know what else to send her with the new drawing. I'm glad Mila's home. I'm not sure I would be able to deal with all of this without her.

* * *

Even though I'm not really dating Court, it hasn't stopped the kids at school from running around gossiping about us getting back together. They believe we are really dating, although we don't do anything a real couple would do. Yes we walk down the hall together, but he doesn't hold my hand or anything to demonstrate we are even a little bit interested in each other. All this gossip doesn't seem to faze Court. He says he doesn't care what people think. I really don't either. At least I think I don't.

To be honest, sometimes I do wish the gossip was real and I could love Court the way I still love Nash. No matter how much I try not to think about him, I do. Hopefully one day I'll wake up and not have the urge to see him. Then maybe my heart will stop aching.

"Emma!" Britney screams running down the hallway. Her cinnamon red hair flows behind her, with her eyes looking as though they are about to burst out of her head.

"What?"

"Ohmigod, Ohmigod, Ohmigod!" She screams jumping up and down.

"What's wrong?" She's starting to scare me.

"Sam-just-called-meeee!"

"Britney take a deep breathe." She tries to recuperate her normal breathing pattern. "Now, Sam called you and said what?" My heart slowly starts to race. Please don't let it be bad news about Nash.

"He told me he got us BAYSIDE TICKETS FOR TONIGHT!" She screams the last couple of words jumping up and down.

"What?! Ohmigod, Ohmigod!" I grab hold of her hands and we both continue to jump as we squeal in excitement, causing everyone around us to stop and stare.

"What's going on?" Court asks joining us.

"We got Bayside tickets." I quickly turn to look at Britney, when I realize she didn't really say she had a ticket for me. "Wait. How many tickets did he get?"

"Four. So Court, if you wanna come with us, you're more than welcome to join us." Britney says putting him on the spot. I wish she had discussed this with me before saying anything.

"Yeah, that sounds cool," Court answers with a huge smile on his face.

"Good. Well I'd better go call Sam to remind him what an awesome boyfriend he is." She walks off to stand by the lockers, which are a few feet away from where we are standing.

"That's exciting. I just got one question for you. Who's Bayside?" Court asks leaning his head against the brick wall.

"They're a punk rock group from Queens. You don't have to go if you don't want to. Britney will understand."

"Are you kidding me? I'm excited. Wait, do you want me to go?"

"Of course." I'm not sure if I really do.

"Good. It'll be our chance to go to another concert together that doesn't involve classical music."

"You're right."

"Anyway, I came to see if you were going to the pep rally today?" He lowers his eyes pitifully, to try to guilt trip me into going.

"Sorry. I know I owe you, but I can't do the pep rally. Please don't make me go."

He starts to laugh. "Okay, I won't. But keep one word in mind, homecoming," he says moving his eyebrows up and down. "See you tonight." He smiles before walking off. What does *homecoming* mean? Oh God, I hope he's not planning on asking me to the dance. Then again, it might be fun. What am I saying, I don't do school dances.

"I told Sam, Court is gonna be joining us," Britney announces walking back.

All of a sudden my heart begins to panic. "Do you think Nash will be there? I know his sister is going." I don't know if I could handle seeing him again.

"I don't think so. I'm sure Sam would've told me, but I can call and ask him."

"No. It's okay."

"Well if he is there, it will just give him more conformation that you're dating Court, which I still don't understand why you're really not. I mean you guys have already slept together," Britney says a little too loud.

"Shhh!" I grab her arm. "I told you, Court and me are just friends, and that's the way we both wanna keep it. So stop pushing the issue."

"Okay, okay." She says rolling her eyes. Sometimes I wish Britney never figured out I had sex. I wish I'd kept it a secret.

I really can't wait for tonight. I just hope my parents will allow me to go. They hate when I don't give them enough notice. I walk into my house with my fingers crossed.

"Emma is that you?" My mother asks walking down the stairs. It looks like she has been napping. Her short hair is all over the place. It's not like my mother to be sleeping in the middle of the day.

"Yeah. Mom, are you okay?"

"Yes. I just dozed off reading a book. How was school?"

"Good."

"Wait, what are you doing here? I thought there was a pep rally today?" She folds her arms under her chest.

"Mom you know I'm not into that kind of stuff."

"Emma, you can't be like that. You need to be there for Court." I really need to tell her the truth about that relationship. Maybe next week I'll explain everything to her, well maybe not everything.

"I know, but I came home to ask you something."

"What?"

"Britney's boyfriend got us tickets to a concert at Cake tonight. Can I go?" I quickly ask.

"Emma, you know I do not like you asking…."

"I know, I know. But I just found out today. Please can I go?"

"Who's going?" She inquisitively asks, raising her right eyebrow higher than her left.

"Britney, her boyfriend Sam, and Court." As soon as I say his name my mother's brown eyes light up.

"Court?"

"Yes. So can I go?"

"Okay."

"Thank you!" I leap to hug her. I'm so excited. All I want to do tonight is have fun. I don't want to think about anything but the music.

"You're welcome." I begin to run up the stairs when my mom says. "Oh by the way, you received a package today. I left it up in your room. I hope you're not spending your money on silly stuff."

"I'm not." I continue to run up the stairs to see what it could be. I don't think I ordered anything.

I open the door to my room and see a medium size perfect square shaped cardboard box on top of my bed. It has my name and address on it, but no return address. Who could've sent me a package?

I grab the scissors off my desk and slice the tape in half. I slowly open the box. I don't know why I always think something is going to jump out at me. I lift the flap and see a letter on top of Nash's black sweatshirt I had returned to him.

I sit on my bed taking deep breaths trying to control all my emotions are rushing through me. I begin to read the letter. Dear Emma,

I know you hate me and you have every reason to. I haven't been good for you. It kills me to know I hurt you, and I wish there was a way I could take everything back. I really meant those words I said to you that day in the rain. I love you in a way I have never loved anyone before. I have so much I need to say to you, including why I kissed Angie, but I would like to do it in person. Please give me a chance to explain.

I love you,

Nash

P.S I can't keep this sweatshirt, it's yours now. If you don't want it throw it out, but I can't keep it without you.

I pull out the sweatshirt, which once again smells like him. I hold it tightly in my arms. I miss him so much it kills me. A piece of paper slips out of my arms. It must have been stuck onto the sweatshirt. I pick it up and see another drawing. This time it's a drawing of our creek. Why is he making it so hard to let him go?

There's a part of me that wishes I never knew anything about his stupid plan or that he kissed Angie. There's also a big part of me wishing I never slept with Court. Lately, I feel like everything I do is full of regrets. I can't live like this anymore.

I look at Nash's sweatshirt and know if I ever want to heal I have to get rid of it. My hands begin to tremble as I try to put it back into the box. Who am I kidding; I can't do this. I know it's the healthy mature thing to do, but I just can't.

I really hope he's not going to be there tonight. I'm not sure I'll be able to stay away from him if he is.

10
Hey, Hey What Can I do

It's good Leo's driving us. I don't think I can concentrate on the road right now. I'm so nervous to see Emma tonight. Sam's already warned me Court will be there tonight. I still don't understand why Mila got Emma two tickets. How in the world am I going to get a chance to talk to her with him there?

I wonder if she received the package I sent her. I was hoping she would call me when she got it, but she hasn't yet. I thought about texting her, but Mila said that wasn't a good idea. She told me to wait for tonight. I hope she's right. I really need tonight to go good, it might be the last chance I get with her.

After getting carded both Johnny and me get bright orange bracelets placed on our wrist. This allows the bartenders to know we are not to be served any type of alcohol. The bouncers warn us not to take them off or we will be kicked out.

As soon as we enter the stairway leading up to the club, I rip mine off and pull out two blue bracelets I kept from the last time Leo, Jen and me were here. I'm not really in the mood to drink, especially after what I did the last time I got drunk, but I like having the option.

I hand one of the bracelets to Johnny. I'm actually starting to like him. Besides, if I can get him on my side, it might be easier to convince Britney I'm not the ass she thinks I am.

The small nightclub is packed. There's a long line of people waiting to check their jackets. We all decide to skip it and head straight for the bar. The brick colored walls are pulsing with the music the unknown opening band is producing on the stage straight across from the bar.

We reach the crowded bar and Mila orders everyone a beer, while I order a Coke. I turn around and stand against the bar and start searching through the crowd for Emma. It's going to be close to impossible to spot her with all the bodies in front of me. I know she's here because I had Sam text me once they arrived.

The opening band says their goodbyes and the DJ begins to play *The Good Life* by Weezer. As people begin to spread out, I try once more to find her, but once again I fail. Maybe she saw me and decided to leave?

Unexpectedly, Leo's elbow strikes me right in the ribs. Before I can question him, he points toward the front of the stage, where Emma is standing. My heart begins to race faster than Jimmy Page's riffs on the guitar. I stand there watching her dance around. I don't see Court, maybe he didn't like the scene and decided to leave.

She looks so beautiful with her skin glowing under the gold and blue lights. She begins to jump and cheer as Bayside takes the stage. She immediately begins to sing along with the band to the song *Sick, Sick, Sick*.

I push off the bar and begin to walk towards her. This is my chance to be near her and remind her how good we are together at concerts. But halfway there, I abruptly stop when I catch sight of Court standing next to her pretending he likes the music.

Why did he have to come? Can't he let her do anything on her own? I turn around and head back to the bar with my insides contorting in fury.

I spend the next three songs standing against the wall staring at them. Every time Court touches her, my skin crawls. She dances around him while he tries unsuccessfully to shake his head to the beat of the song. He really is an ass.

Suddenly, Emma stops dancing and whispers something in his ear. He turns to walk towards the back, but she pulls his arm to stop him. Did she see me staring at them? Maybe he's coming back here to confront me. She says something to him while nodding her head. She then forms a beautiful smile, and begins to walk straight towards the other side of the bar.

Here's my chance. This time nothing is stopping me from talking to her. Each step I take towards her causes my heart to race a notch faster. "Hi," I say reaching her side.

Her amber brown eyes pop open when she realizes it's me. "Hi." She tersely turns back to face the bar.

"Are you having fun?"

She nods.

"Did you receive the package I sent you?"

She nods again.

"Do you think maybe we can go outside for a minute to talk?" Please let her say yes.

"Can I help you?" The stupid bartender asks, interrupting us."

"Two waters please," she anwers.

"Two waters coming up."

I'll try again, hopefully this time she'll answer or at least nod again. "So, do you wanna go…."

"Not now," she says, still staring at the bartender. Okay, she didn't say no. This could be a good sign.

"Eight dollars." The bartender hands her two Poland Spring bottles.

"I got it," I say, pulling out my wallet.

She finally turns to face me with an endearing smile and says, "Thank you." She then turns back towards the stage and heads back to Court.

I produce a small grin that quickly grows into a huge smile. I think I might be getting to her.

"So, does this smile mean things just went well with Emma?" Mila asks, joining me at the bar.

"Kind of. I really think if I can spend a few more minutes with her, I can get her to remember why she picked me the first time around."

"Then why don't you go to her?"

"Because Court is with her. Remember you got him a ticket? He won't let me get anywhere near her," I say, watching Emma disappear into the crowd.

I turn to face Mila just in time to see her form a wicked smile as her eyes narrow. "Leave it to me. I have an idea. I'll be right back." She walks off towards the bathroom and stops Sam from entering. Whatever her plan is, I hope it works. I need it to work.

* * *

I walk back towards Court with my legs shaking so hard I feel like I'm on one of those suspended bridges you find in a playground. Bayside is performing their hearts out, but I can't hear a sound they are making.

My heart is about to burst out of my chest. Seeing Nash sent tingles throughout my each of my limbs. I tried so hard to be strong back at the bar. I knew if he asked me one more time to go outside with him, I would've said yes.

I hand Court his water bottle with my hand trembling. "Are you okay?" He asks.

"Yeah, just thirsty." I take the bottle and take a long gulp. I try to get back into the music Bayside is performing but I can't. All I can do is think about Nash's golden green eyes and the way he looked at me. I turn back to see if I can find him, but I can't.

"Hey! This is the best concert ever!" Britney yells, over the loud music that is now making it's way into my eardrums.

"Where's Sam?" I ask. She and Sam had disappeared as soon as the opening band went off the stage.

"Bathroom."

I turn to look at Court, who is doing his best to pretend to like the music. He's nodding his head to the unfamiliar rhythms. He's such an amazing person for coming out tonight. I need to stop thinking about Nash and only worry about having a good time with Court. I owe it to him.

Seconds later, Sam comes back to join us with a weary look on his face. He tugs at the end of the sleeves of his navy blue and red striped sweater, and with trepidation in his voice says, "Umm…Court…umm, do you think I can talk to you outside for a minute? Both Britney and me glance at each other in confusion. What happened to Sam in the bathroom?

"Yeah, is everything cool?" Court asks as puzzled as we are.

"Yeah, I just need your advice on something. It's important."

"What is it? Is it about me?" Britney asks looking concerned.

"No, no. It's just a guy thing."

"Ok. Will you be alright?" Court asks me.

"Yeah, don't worry." He gives me a baffled look right before he heads outside with Sam.

"What was that all about?" I ask Britney.

Before Britney can answer, the last person I expect to see again interrupts us. Mila stands in front of us looking beautiful in her patchwork halter-top and flare jeans. She really does look like a hippie from the 1960's.

"I don't know why seeing her also gets my heart racing. "I thought I saw you guys here. Are you guys having fun?" She says loud enough for even the band to hear.

"Yeah!" We both say.

"Hey. Is my brother here with you?" Britney asks her. I can't believe Johnny is hanging out with her. It's so weird how everyone in my life seems to have a connection to Nash. I'm never going to be able to remove him from my life.

"Yeah. Listen, I actually came over here because I need your help."

"My help?" Britney asks pointing to herself.

"Yeah. Just come to the bathroom with me.

"Yeah sure. Come on Emma."

"Actually can it just be you. It's something personal and I really don't know Emma like that. I'm sorry."

"It's okay," I say trying not to let her know her rejection hurts. When did Britney and her become such great friends anyway? I feel like I'm being left out of everything.

"I'll be right back," Britney says and walks off with Mila leaving me all by myself among a sea of unrecognizable faces.

I try to sway my body to the music and pretend I don't care I'm standing here alone. I sing along with the crowd to the song *Masterpiece*, while I stroke a strip of my hair by my neck as I shift my weight from my left leg to my right leg. I really hope Court comes back soon.

Without warning, two hands land on my waist. The smell of my favorite cologne tells me it's Nash without even having to look back. What is he doing? My body shakes from thrill and fear.

My eyes close as I try to take this moment in. He brings his body closer to mine making my skin rise with goose bumps. His hands begin to slowly stroke my sides, as his warm breath lands across my neck. The heat of his chest against my back burns me with desire. I fight each muscle in my body not to turn around and just fall into his arms.

He brings his lips to my left ear and whispers, "I miss you so much."

I open my eyes and realize I can't do this. I can't let this happen. Nash turns me around and with sincerity in his eyes he begins to say, "Emma I lo...."

I put my hand on his chest to stop him from talking. "I'm sorry but I can't do this right now." I walk away from him feeling anger in my heart, but not towards him. I'm angry with myself for walking away from him, when I all want to do is stay in his arms.

I run right into Court who's walking back in with Sam. "Whoa, are you alright?" He asks catching me in his arms before I fall backwards.

"I want to go home."

"Are you okay?"

"Yes. I just wanna go home. Please let's just go home."

Court's eyes narrow as he notices Nash standing in the crowd. "Did he do anything to you?"

"No. He has nothing to do with this. Can we go now?" I need to get out of here before I turn around and run back into Nash's arms.

"Sure." Court places his hand on my back and leads me to the coat check counter.

I need to be strong. I can't let what I'm feeling control me. I turn around and spot Nash staring at me with pain spilled all over his face. I wish he wasn't looking at me that way.

I turn back to put on my hoody and then can't help but look over at Nash once again. The pain in his face diminishes and begins to be replaced by his gorgeous crooked smile when he realizes I am wearing his sweatshirt. I smile right back before I walk out of Cake with Court.

11
I Can't Quit You Baby

I've been consumed with images of Emma in my sweatshirt all weekend long. I close my eyes and still smell her sweet scent. I can feel the warmth of her body up against mine. I really feel like I might have a chance to get her back this time around.

I wanted to call her or maybe send her a text message, but once again Mila suggested I wait. She said, instead I should show up at her school at the end of the day and surprise her. Since Mila's ideas have worked out great so far, I've decided to take her advice.

I jump on my bike and decide to skip my last class. I'm sure one day of missing out on physics notes won't hurt me. Besides, Roxy's in that class too and I'm sure she'll fill me in on what I missed.

Sam informed me Emma drove her mom's car to school today. So I'm going to park my bike in front of it and hope she doesn't run away when she sees me.

The cool September air is making me regret taking my motorcycle instead of my truck. I guess I thought if she sees my bike she'd remember all the good times we had on it.

I zoom from row to row looking for her silver Toyota. I think I must have missed it, because I don't see it anywhere. Maybe she already left school. I turn my handles to drive through the parking lot once more but stop before I move an inch. Yes! I have finally found it parked near one of the exits.

I pull up in front of her car and try to find a way to look cool. I sit sideways on my bike with my legs stretched out in front of me. I can't stand how nervous I am. There's a crawly feeling in my stomach I've never felt before. I wonder if this is what it means to have butterflies in your stomach?

Damn, what if she refuses to talk to me? Or worse, she walks out with Court and he wants to start a fight. I'm ready if he does. I've been dying to hit him again. What am I saying? I can't hit him. Emma would never speak to me again if I do.

The doors swing open and the students of Cypress Oak High School begin to spill out, all of them looking relieved to be out of school. I know exactly how they all feel. I personally can't wait to graduate and start my real life. I hope Emma will be with me when I do.

So many different faces are walking towards me which makes it hard to find Emma. Just as I'm about to give up, I catch a glimpse of her walking out into the sunlight. Every time I see her, my heart beats a little faster. She's so beautiful.

Britney is the first to notice me. She takes he elbow and nudges Emma on her left arm and motions toward me with her big head. Fear explodes throughout my entire body. Please don't let her reject me. I might not be able to recover this time.

Emma doesn't look upset to see me, but she doesn't look too happy either. I try to smile hoping I can look confident and maybe get her to smile back, but all I manage to produce is a weak grin.

"What are you doing here?" She asks, tucking her hair behind her left ear. I love when she does that.

"I thought maybe we can have that talk now."

"She does not want to talk to you! When are you gonna get that" Britney chimes in. "Leave her the hell alo…."

"Brit, I think this is my choice," Emma says and then turns to me. "Yeah we can go for that talk now." My weak grin now becomes a big smile.

"Emma! You can't!" Damn it! Why can't Britney just shut her mouth?

"It's okay. I need to do this. I'll be okay."

"Fine! Call me later." Britney makes sure to give me the evil eye before she walks away. I'm going to have to do something to get that girl back on my side again.

"You ready?" I ask.

She finally smiles and says, "Yeah." She jumps on the back of my bike and wraps her arms around me sending chills up and down my spine. I start the engine and take off. I know exactly where to take her. It's the only place I know we can really talk.

* * *

The cool air slaps my face making it hard to breathe. I still can't believe I agreed to go with him. The truth is I can no longer stay away from him. Everyone keeps telling me it's going get better, but it hasn't yet.

Every morning I wake up with every part of me aching for him. I find myself thinking about him every minute of the day. I wonder where he is and what he's thinking. I'm tired of feeling this way. That's why I have to talk to him today. I need to see if there is still something there to hold on to. Or has too much damage occurred to prevent us from being together.

Nash drives through curves and hills making my stomach spin with exhilaration. I squeeze my arms around his waist. I forgot how scary and free it feels to ride behind him. I know exactly where he's taking me.

We pull up to our creek, the place that became our own personal paradise over the summer. The trees were once filled with green leaves are now full of gold and red ones. They seem to be happy we have returned as they sway back and forth.

Nash hops off his bike first and then helps me off. I remove my helmet, and shake my hair loose. His hand brushes against my skin, which makes every cell in my body fill with elation.

I feel like a Popsicle. I wish he had brought his truck instead. The soft wind makes me shiver even more and yearn for some heat from Nash's body.

We begin to walk to the edge of the creek. The crunch of the dried leaves under our feet flows in the air. "I'm really happy you finally agreed to talk," he says.

"I thought it was about time we got everything out in the open." I'm having a hard time looking him in the eyes, knowing I have a big secret to reveal myself.

"You're right. I guess I should begin. First of all I need to say how sorry I am for everything I put you through this summer. I was so wrong to use you. You have to believe me when I say my intention was never to hurt you."

"What did you think I was going to feel when you were done with your stupid revenge scheme?" Anger starts to fill my heart again.

"I don't know. I was so blinded by getting Court back, I didn't think. But you need to know when I told you I loved you it was true. It still is true. My heart had been dead with all that happened with my brother Ben and Angie, until you came into my life." Nash closes his eyes, takes a deep breath in, and continues. "Before you came into my life, I was just existing. Not really caring about anything. But then I met you and everything changed. You made me want to laugh again. You made me look forward to another day. All I wanted to do was spend every moment I could with you."

"All you wanted to do was make Court suffer."

"No. Yes I'll admit I got a kick out of seeing Court broken up over things, but he wasn't the reason I spent so many moments with you. He's not the reason we came up here all the time just to talk. I really miss talking to you." He takes another deep breath and with agony in his eyes he continues, "Emma I miss you so much it's slowly killing me inside." I want to believe everything he's saying, but something is holding me back.

"But what about Angie?" I choke up trying to stop myself from crying. I'm not going to lose my strength to a bunch of tears right now.

"There is nothing going on between Angie and me. The picture you saw was of Angie kissing me. I'm not going to lie, I kissed her back but only to try to forget you were with Court. I quickly pushed her away after only a few seconds and told her I was in love with you. Look, I know you're with Court now and maybe there will never…."

"I'm not with Court," I utter.

He snaps his head up with relieving pleasure taking over his face. "You guys broke up?"

"No. We were never back together."

"What? But…."

"I wanted you to believe I had moved on. Court agreed to pretend because…."

"He wanted to see me hurt this time."

"No, because he's a good friend to me."

"I'm sorry. Do you want him to be more than that?" Nash asks looking sadly away from me again.

"No," I whisper.

"What do you want? Because the only thing I want is you back in my life," he says looking up at me again, making my heart melt.

A huge part of me wants to jump in his arms and tell him there's nothing more I want too, but there's another part of me that's scared of getting hurt again. "I'm not sure I can put my heart through this again," I say finally giving in to my tears.

"If you give me another chance I promise to protect your heart with all I have." He takes a step closer to me and I swear I can feel both of our hearts beating at the same rapid pace. "I promise to never hurt you again. I will prove to you that you can trust me again."

I look down at the rusted colored leaves on the ground. I'm afraid if I look into his eyes I won't be able to say no any longer. He places his warm hand under my chin, tilts my head up, and says, "Emma I love you, and if you say no, I won't bother you anymore. But if you say yes, I will spend every day doing what I can to deserve your love." He closes his eyes and with fear in his voice he asks, "Will you give me another chance?"

My mind comes up with a dozen reasons why I should say no, but I ignore all of them and say, "Yes."

Nash's eyes shoot open and my favorite smile appears on his beautiful face. He bridges the gap between us and just looks into my eyes making my heart fill with anticipation. I can't believe this is happening. We are back together.

Nash brings his soft warm lips to mine and begins to kiss me. My body immediately melts into his as warmth begins to remove all the cold I had been feeling. This is all I've wanted for the last few weeks.

All that anger I had been holding on to no longer exists inside of me. I am truly happy. I can't help but think Jason had something to do with all of this. In my mind he's become my guardian angel sending good things my way.

"You don't know how happy I am," Nash says when we pull apart.

"Me too."

"I promise to always be honest with you and never have secrets between us," Nash says, crashing my heart. I have to tell him about what I did with Court. I open my mouth and try to find the right words, but I can't find them. I don't want to ruin this moment.

Nash drops me off at the school parking lot, just as the sun begins its journey to the other side of the world. I get off his bike feeling whole again. I kiss him goodbye and watch him drive off. I still can't believe he's back in my life.

"What are you still doing here?" Court asks startling me.

"A…a I had stuff to do. What are you doing?"

"Just finished football practice. I'm actually glad I found you, I have something to ask you…."

"Yeah, I have to talk to you too." I have to let him know Nash is back in my life. I just hope he doesn't flip.

114

"Me first. I know this is short notice but I wanted to know if you'd go to the homecoming dance with me next Friday? I wanted to ask you in some outrageous way, but I know you wouldn't have liked that. Besides Britney told me I better ask you today."

"What?" Ohmigod, why is he asking me to homecoming? Why now? How am I supposed to tell him no and then tell him about Nash at the same time?

"I know you don't do school dances, but I talked to Britney who said she'd go with Sam. So the four of us can go together. She also told me not to take no for an answer. So come on, say you'll go to homecoming with me."

"Don't you have someone else you'd rather go with? I'm sure there's a line of girls that'll go with you."

"But I don't wanna go with them. I want to go with you," he smiles and quickly adds, "As friends. Come on, that way I don't have to worry about how the date is gonna end, or try too hard to impress some girl."

What am I supposed to say? I can't say yes. Why did Britney tell him to ask me? Note to self, must kill Britney later. I swear she's going to pay.

"Come on, you're really killing my ego. Just say yes, I promise we'll have fun."

"Okay," I say without thinking. He scoops me up and twirls me around.

"Good. Okay I gotta get home. We'll talk more about this later. Oh wait, you had something to tell me," Court says looking at me with his sweet baby blue eyes.

Okay Emma, you can do this. Just tell him Nash is back in your life. "It's nothing important. We'll talk later." I know I'm being a big chicken. I get in my car and begin to freak out.

My hands grip the steering wheel so hard my fingers are beginning to cramp up. Why did I agree to go with him? I have to tell him the truth. He deserves that and more. That's it, I'll call him as soon as I get home and explain everything to him. He has to understand. At least I hope he understands.

I open the door just in time to hear my father say, "You're going to do whatever the hell you want without thinking about the rest of us!" He storms out of the kitchen looking like he's about to blow fire out of his nose. My mother follows him with a stern look on her face.

"What's going on?" I ask, not sure if I really want to know.

I don't know why I thought they would smile and try to reassure me everything is fine; instead they both turn their anger towards me. "Where have you been? Did it ever occur to you, I might need my car?" My mother asks putting her hands on her hips.

"I'm sorry I was…."

"And why do you even have a cell phone if you're not going to use it?" My father chirps in.

"I…I was…." I can't tell them the truth, they'll flip out and might not let me see Nash again. "I was talking to Court, he asked me to homecoming."

"Oh my God!" My mother squeals coming to hug me. "I can't believe my baby girl is going to homecoming." She gives me another hug. "Oh my God, we have to go dress shopping."

"Mom, really it's not a big deal. I can just wear something….."

"Not a big deal? This is a huge deal. I always wanted to go to homecoming but never got the chance. I'm so happy you are not living the same life I lived in high school." Oh great she's going to try to live vicariously through me again.

What have I just done? I can't cancel on Court now. Great, I just got back together with Nash and I already might lose him.

12
Everyday is a Winding Road

I feel like a different person than I was a couple of hours ago. It's like the world is new again. I still can't believe Emma and me are back together, and I get to hold her again. This time I'm going to do everything right. I have this new energy in my life and it feels good. I even feel like doing some schoolwork.

"What are you doing?" Mila asks, walking into my room. I'm so happy it doesn't even bother me that she didn't knock first.

"Calculus, and you?"

"I have to go to work soon. I got a bartending job at Cake."

"Congrats. Does that mean it'll be easier for me to get drinks there now?" I ask laughing.

"Not a chance. I would like to keep this job. Especially now that mom is insisting I start contributing. I knew her loving, caring mom act would soon end."

"Oh God, please don't tell me you two are gonna start fighting again?" I can't handle it if they do.

"I'm not starting anything. Mom is always gonna blame me for Ben joining the army. She doesn't care that I was totally against it. All she cares about is that I made that stupid comment a month prior to him joining. How did I know he was going to take it serious? It was a joke. Telling him to join the army was only a joke. I didn't think he would do it." Mila's cool and collective persona disappears and she becomes vulnerable and small while remembering.

"It's not your fault he joined. You didn't make that choice for him."

"I know. Look whatever, let's talk about something else." And just like that, she shuts herself off and goes back to pretending she's good. My family is great at burying away any painful reminders of Ben deep inside. "Anyway, what's new with you?"

I try my best not to smile, as I say, "Nothing."

She eyes me suspiciously while she inspects me from top to bottom. She puts her hands on her hips and says, "What's going on?"

"What do you mean?"

"You look different. You look happy. Did something happen with Emma?"

The corners of my mouth rise even higher. "Yeah, we're back together."

"What?" She jumps on the bed next to me. "How did this happen? I want to know everything."

I tell her the whole story. Watching the enjoyment in her eyes makes me even more excited of what's happening between Emma and me.

"Oh little brother, I'm so happy for you. Now don't fuck this up again." She warns.

"I won't. I'm in love with her and I'm not gonna mess this up again."

"Did I just hear what I think I heard?" My mother asks walking into my room with frustration in her eyes. I didn't even realize she arrived.

"Yeah, you heard correctly," I state. I'm not hiding my relationship any more.

"What about Angie? Are you ready to throw away what you had with her?"

"What Angie and I had has been over for a long time now. Mom you have to deal with the fact that I'm never getting back together with her again."

"You are just like your damn father! Well, I'm telling you this right now, that girl is not welcomed in my house!"

"Whatever!"

"Nash, I swear to God if I see her here…."

"Mom, enough! He gets it," Mila says interrupting her.

I wish my mom would let go of the anger she has towards my dad. I hate when she says, I'm just like him. I'm nothing like him. I would never abandon my family when they needed me the most. I didn't walk away from Angie; she walked away from me.

"I need a fucking drink. I swear the both of you are…." She storms out before she can finish her sentence.

"Does mom know Angie is the one who cheated on you last year?"

"Nah."

"Maybe if you tell her she'll be…."

"No. I really don't care what Mom thinks. I'm with Emma now and it doesn't matter what anybody thinks. Nothing is gonna come between us again."

* * *

I woke up this morning feeling happiness I haven't felt in a long time, but at the same time my stomach is twisted in horrible knots. I have no idea what I'm going to do about homecoming next week. I need to tell Court the truth about Nash and me and then maybe he'll want to go with somebody else.

"Why didn't you answer my texts last night?" Britney asks, meeting me at my locker.

"'Cause I was not in the mood to talk to you. Why didn't you warn me that Court was going to ask me to homecoming? And why did you tell him you and Sam would join us? As long as I've known you, you have never wanted to go to a school dance."

"Well I thought it would be cool to go this year. Besides, I thought maybe a romantic school dance would show you that you belong with Court and not that asshole Nash."

"Well it's too late. I'm back with Nash."

"What?" She asks slamming my locker door shut. "Are you stupid or something? Do you not remember what he did to you?"

"Yeah, but we talked…Britney, I just have to give Nash and me another chance. I don't know why you can't understand that?"

"Because I'm the one who watched you fall apart when you learned what an ass he is. I can't watch you go through that again."

"Don't worry you won't have to. I believe Nash when he says he won't hurt me again."

"I hope you're right. So, what are you going to do about Court?"

"I have to tell him the truth. I just hope he'll still want to be my friend."

"There you are!" Court says, walking up behind us and putting his arm around Britney and me.

"Hey Court! What's up?" Britney asks looking at me with her olive green eyes filled with worry.

"I just bought the tickets for homecoming. Tell Sam I got yours too. He asked me to buy them last night."

"Wait. You and Sam spoke last night?" I ask confused. Did Sam tell him Nash and me are back together? No, he would look more upset, I think.

"Well more like texted. He asked me to buy the tickets. He didn't want Britney paying for them."

"He's so sweet," Britney says with pure bliss in her voice. "Well I'd better get to Math class before Mr. Jackson gives me detention for being late again. She walks away leaving me alone with Court, and giving me the chance I need to say everything that is trapped inside of me.

"Umm…Court I really need to talk to you." My heart is beating so fast I swear it's going to take off out of my body.

"What's up?"

"I…I need to tell you something and I hope after I tell you this we can still be…."

"Yo Court, coach is looking for you. He said it's important," Adam says interrupting us.

"Alright, I'll be right there," he calls out while Adam continues to walk down the crowded hallway. "So what do you need to tell me?" He looks at me with his eyes full of hope.

I really don't want to say anything that can hurt him. "Nothing. Just go see your coach."

"Okay. Um…Emma?"

"Yeah?"

"I'm really glad we're friends again, and that you're going with me to homecoming. I hope whatever you have to tell me won't crush that." For a second there, I believe he's figured it out. "Let's just have fun next Friday. Okay?"

"Okay." I'm going to have to tell Nash I'm going with Court.

The past week has gone by so slow. At home my mother has been on cloud nine since I told her about homecoming. She and my dad seem to be out of their funk, which is a good thing. I was really getting tired of not knowing what was going on.

My mother did make me go dress shopping with her. She kept picking out pink dresses, while I kept picking for black ones. My choice finally won, since I paid for it myself. I still have all the money I made this summer, which I hope soon will be used towards a car. But every time I bring it up my parents turn on their selective hearing. Here I thought only teenagers had that ability?

Anyway, Nash has had to work all week long so we haven't been able to see each other. We only talk on the phone at night right before I go to bed. I haven't told him about homecoming yet. I want to do it when I see him. I'm hoping if he has me in front of him, it will be harder for him to get mad.

Since my parents still think I'm dating Court, I'm having Nash pick me up at Britney's house. He should be here any minute for our official first date. I'm so nervous. My stomach feels like it's being twisted, jabbed, and squeezed all at the same time.

"The jerk is here." Britney says coming into her room with a spoon full of peanut butter. I have no idea how she can eat it without chocolate attached to it.

"Will you stop calling him that."

"Did you tell him about homecoming yet?"

"No. I'm telling him tonight. Tell Sam I said thank you for not saying a word."

"No prob. Well if you need anything, like someone to come and rescue you, just call me."

No matter how mad she's making me at the moment, Britney always says the perfect thing to make me smile and remind me why we are best friends. "Thank you." I give her a tight hug before I walk out into her living room.

Nash and Johnny are sitting on the couch talking about tattoos. It's weird to see the guy I was once madly in love with when I was a kid talking to the guy I'm in love with now.

"Hey," Nash says, making his famous crooked smile that makes my heart race wildly.

"Hey."

"You ready to go?"

"Yeah."

"Well you kids have fun, but not too much fun. You know what I'm saying?" Johnny says to Nash with a hard expression.

Nash starts laughing. "Same goes to you when you go out with my sister."

We both laugh harder walking out of Britney's house. I hope this happy moment can continue when I tell Nash everything.

13
A Matter of Time

Emma's perfume floats by my nose causing vibes of excitement to jump from nerve ending to nerve ending. One of the things I love most about her is she doesn't need much to look incredible. She doesn't need a pound of makeup, or the other crap girls use to feel good about themselves. Her red sweater and jeans is enough to take my breath away.

We sit in my truck without saying a word, just listening to the band Conditions sing *Sweet Disposition* on the radio. Her hand rests on her lap tapping to the beat of the music. I want to reach over and grab it, but I'm not sure how to. It's been so easy to talk to her over the phone for the past week, but now having her sit next to me, I'm finding it difficult to say anything. I'm afraid to say something wrong and send her running again.

"So where are we going?" She asks, looking as nervous as I am.

"I thought we'd go get some dinner. Do you like Italian food?"

"I love it."

She bites her lower lip and keeps looking out her window. Maybe she's regretting giving me a second chance? I wish I knew what was going through her head.

"How's school?" I ask trying to make conversation.

"It's okay. Lots of homework, what about you? How's senior year treating you?"

"Good. My classes are pretty easy. I can't wait to get out and start my tattoo apprenticeship."

"I bet. It must be great to know what you want to do with your life. I wish I had some idea."

"You still have time to figure it out. Just know whatever it is, I'll be here supporting you one hundred percent."

She smiles making my heart pump a little harder. I pull into Trinos, a small Italian restaurant in Monticello. "You ready to eat?"

"Um…yeah." I put my hand on my door handle and I'm about to pull it open, when I hear her say, "Nash wait." I knew there was something bothering her.

I turn to face her and see her beautiful smile is no longer present on her face. My heart now pumps with fear.

"I need to talk to you first."

"What's wrong?" Something tells me, whatever it is, it's going to sting.

She tucks her hair behind her left ear and says in one breath, "I'm going to the homecoming dance with Court next Friday."

Did I hear her right? Did she say she's going to a dance with Court? Any ounce of happiness I had has just evaporated into thin air. "What?"

"Next Friday, I'm going to my school homecoming dance with Court. He asked me to go as friends, and I said yes. I'm really sorry I didn't tell you sooner."

Anger penetrates my body making every muscle in my body turn rock hard. How can this be happening? "Does he know we're back together?"

"No. I haven't told him yet."

"What? Why not? I don't get it Emma, do you wanna be with me or what?"

"I do." Tears begin to run down her face. I want to kick myself for making her cry, but at the same time I can't help being mad.

"Court has been a really good friend to me, and I owe him a lot. When he asked me to the dance, I felt like I had no choice but to say yes. And then when my mom got excited about the news, I knew it was going to be impossible to cancel."

"I can't believe this." Why does it have to be so hard to be with her?

* * *

The rage filling Nash's eyes is scaring me. Any minute he's going to turn around and tell me I'm not worth it. Then he'll run off to be with Angie.

"I know you're mad, but I wanted to be honest with you."

"I'm trying not to be mad, but how would you feel if I told you I was going to a dance with Angie?"

"I understand if you want this to be over," I utter softly.

"What?" He looks shocked I'd even suggest it. "No. Emma I finally got you back in my life. I'm not going to let something like a school dance ruin it." He takes a deep breath, "Are you sure you're only going as friends?"

"Yes. Court and I have only been friends since we broke up." I know I should tell him about what happened in the Hamptons, but I can't. It would be too much for him to deal with right now.

"I guess then, I'm cool with it." His words might say he's okay but his eyes tell me another story. "Just promise me you won't have any fun."

I let out a nervous laugh. "At a school dance? Not a problem."

He sits straight back against the seat pressing his head up against the headrest. With his eyes closed he takes another deep breath. I want to find the perfect words to say that'll make all of this better, but I can't find them.

Nash turns his head and stares into my eyes, and then lifts his hand up to softly caress my face. This touch is exactly what I need. "I love you, and I trust you." He leans forward and kisses me making me feel secure again.

I want to be excited, but the part of me that still fears the worst, won't let me relax. I know somewhere deep down Nash is having second thoughts about our relationship.

My whole school has homecoming fever. All everyone does is talk about it. Years before, I never really paid any attention to it. This was always the time Jason and me would be planning his birthday. This year it falls on the day after homecoming. It's still so strange he's not here to celebrate what would have been his seventeenth birthday.

I miss him so much. I'm going to go visit his grave on Saturday. I asked Nash if he would come with me and he said yes. I'm glad he agreed, because I'm not sure I will be able to keep it together without him.

Jason would be laughing his head off at the thought of me going to the homecoming dance. He especially would get a kick out of all the rumors Christy is circulating. His favorite one would be the one about me paying Court to take me. I can't believe people actually believe them.

Christy's hatred has increased since Court and me have become friends again. She spends every English class glaring at me. If looks could hurt me, I would be all black and blue by now. I just smile at her, knowing that it kills her. But inside, I'm shaking with fear. I know sooner or later the truth about Nash and me will be out and it might send Court running to her again. I hope not, but it's a big possibility.

I wish I could say things with Nash have been perfect since we had our talk, but they haven't. He hasn't really brought up the dance again, but I can tell it's bothering him. I give him credit though, because if it was the other way around I don't think I would be this understanding.

Now, the night before the dance I'm meeting up with him to spend some time together and make sure he is really okay with everything.

We drive down to the diner where we ate our first meal together. It was the day I knew everything in my life was going to change. It was also the day I came home to end my relationship with Court.

"I'm glad you didn't have to work," I say, munching on fries.

"Yeah, well I traded with Mila so I can work tomorrow. I rather be at the cafe than sit at home thinking about you and Court at the dance." I can hear the agony in his voice.

"Nothing is going to happen. Besides Sam will be with us, and if you want, you can ask him to give you a full report."

"No. It's not necessary. I trust you. It's Court I don't trust."

"For the last time, he and I are just friends."

"I know. Okay enough about the dance. I just wanna enjoy each other." He takes my hand into his and gives it a firm squeeze. I wish there was a way to make this easier for him.

We enjoy our date together, but behind his smile, I can tell his mind is going crazy with thoughts. I walk out of the diner thinking we might go somewhere else, but quickly learn that's not going to happen when Nash says, "Well I'd better take you home."

I nod, because I'm afraid if I try to say something my voice will crack.

Nash keeps both of his hands on the cold steering wheel. His breathing becomes heavier with each exit we pass. "So what color is your dress?"

"Black."

"Are you guys taking a limo?" He asks focusing his eyes on the dark road.

"No. Court is driving us."

"That's right, he has that fancy car. Who needs a limo when you have a Mercedes?"

I can't help but feel defeated. I think Nash can feel my pain because he quickly says, "I'm sorry. I know I keep saying I'm cool with everything, but the truth is I'm not."

"Nash, I swear nothing is going to happen with Court."

"It's not that you're going with Court that's bothering me."

"Then what's bothering you?"

"It's that I wish I was taking you to your dance." He turns his head to look at me and says, "I want to be the one who gets to see you in your new dress and gets to take pictures with you. I want to be the one who gets to dance all night with you. It sucks. I'm sorry I feel this way." He parks his truck at the top of my street.

A lump scorches my throat. "I wish you were the one that was taking me too." I know exactly what I have to do to make this right. "How about it if we did get to dance?"

"What?" Nash asks crinkling his forehead.

"How about you meet me after the dance? My parents are letting me stay out extra late that night for the after party. I wasn't planning on going, but they don't have to know that. How about you meet me after the dance?"

"What about Court?"

"I'll explain it to him. It's about time he learns the truth."

"Are you sure?"

"Nash, don't you know all I want to do is be with you. I don't care anymore who knows. So will you meet me after the dance?"

"Of course I will. I can't wait." Nash pulls me into his arms and begins to kiss me. I can't wait either. I just hope this is not a mistake.

14
Homecoming

Instead of going straight home, I decide to drive to the Free Bird café and go talk to Mila, who is covering my shift. This whole dance thing is sitting heavy on my mind. I've been going crazy since Emma told me she was going with Court to the stupid dance. I wish the asshole would get out of our life already.

I walk into the Free Bird Café, which Jimmy the owner, has made into a 1969 inspired café. There are murals of all the artists who performed at the Woodstock festival covering each wall, and all the chairs and long bench cushions are covered in tie-dye fabric. Lava lamps sit all over the café, and everything on the menu is named after an artist or song from that time.

You would think Jimmy had been at the Woodstock festival and is trying to hold on to his glory days, but he wasn't even born back then. He actually came into this world almost a decade later. He's just a product of growing up around here and knowing the only huge event to happen around here still brings in a huge amount of money.

To my surprise, I spot Roxy sitting at the counter laughing at something Mila is saying. They both turn to look at me, and smile.

"What? You had to come by and check out what you're missing out on?" Mila asks, serving some big trucker looking guy a fancy sandwich.

"What's going on?" Roxy says, getting up to give me a hug.

"Nothing. How are you?"

"Pretty good. Taking a night off from my son Ryder. By the way, I should warn you, I'm not here alone."

"Who's here with you?" I ask afraid of the answer. Please don't let it be who I think it is.

"Angie. She's in the bathroom." Damn it! I knew it. I've been trying to avoid her at school, and I knew sooner or later she would show up here or at my house. "She thought you were working tonight."

"Let me guess, my mom told her that."

"You guessed it. Anyway, before she comes out tell me how your date with Emma." Mila asks.

Roxy twirls so fast on her stool, she almost falls off. "What? You're back with Emma?"

"Yeah." I didn't want her to know yet. She wasn't so supportive the first time around.

"What about Court? I thought they were back together?" Roxy says pushing her platinum blond hair back.

"No they're not. They're just friends."

"There's no such thing. Trust me, that boy is trying to get into her pants. And he's really good at getting what he wants," Angie says laughing, causing chills to go up and down my spine.

I slowly turn around and see her standing behind me in another very revealing top. I know she puts these shirts on hoping to draw my attention. A few months ago I would have taken her straight to my truck to have some fun, but now all I want is for her to leave me alone. "What are you doing here?" I ask, ignoring what she just said.

"Your mom told me you were working tonight, so I thought I'd come see you since you don't seem to want to answer my calls or texts."

"Maybe it's 'cause I don't wanna talk to you."

"Why?"

"Angie go home," I say taking a seat next to Roxy.

"Is it 'cause that stupid girl is back in your life? You're so stupid. She's never going to love you the way...."

"Shut up!" I yell. I can't listen to her crap any longer.

She steps closer to me with sadness in her eyes and says, "Fine. But don't forget I'm the one that was there for you when your life was falling apart, not her. I'm still in love you, but I don't know how much longer I'm gonna be here waiting for you." She turns around and storms off.

Roxy turns to face me and begins, "Nash, are you sure about this? Emma and you don't...."

"Stay out of it! I wanna be with her and that's all that matters. I don't care what anybody thinks."

"You're right. But I'm warning you, you'd better not hurt her again," Roxy says getting up.

"I won't."

"Good." She nods, as somewhat of a smile forms on her face. "Well, I better go check on Angie. I'll see you guys later. Bye."

"Bye," both Mila and me say simultaneously.

"Wow, that was intense. So, what's going on? Is everything okay with Emma?" Mila asks pouring me a cup of coffee.

"I guess. She said she wants me to meet her after the dance."

"Well that's good. Right?"

"Yeah, but it still pisses me off she gets to spend the first half of the night with Court. What if she realizes...."

"Stop it. When are you going to get it through your thick skull she wants to be with you?" She puts her hands on the counter and gives me a stern look as she says, "She chose you in the summer and she's choosing you now. So stop thinking you're still in competition with Court." I know she's right, but my male-ego is still apprehensive.

"Now instead of worrying about her being at a stupid school dance, why don't you come up with something to do after the dance that will blow her mind. Something that'll show her that choosing you was the right choice," Mila says walking towards the other end of the counter to help a new customer who just walked in.

"You're right." I do have to do something to make her forget all about that stupid dance, and I think I know exactly what I should do. "Umm...Mila do you think you could cover my shift tomorrow night too."

She stops to stare at me with disbelief and shakes her head no as she says, "You're lucky I love you, and I need the money. Now you'd better go before I change my mind."

"Thanks sis. I owe you one!"

"Yes you do!" She yells as I rush out the door.

I'm going to make tomorrow a night Emma will never forget.

135

* * *

Court was amazing on the football field. He scored two touchdowns while I was there. I haven't cheered that loud in a long time. It reminded me of being a kid and watching football games with my father. We'd always rooted for the NY Giants. As I got older, I began to lose interest since none of my friends, including Jason, were into sports.

I still can't believe I remembered all the rules. I tried to explain what was going on to Britney, but all she understood was a touchdown meant the team made six points and a field goal after the touchdown gave them one more point.

We were really having a good time and I wish we could have stayed for the whole game, but my mother insisted I come home early to get ready for the dance.

Britney also agreed to get ready at my house since her mother had to work and would not be home to help her. She did ask for pictures as proof. She can't believe her anti-school event daughter is actually going to a school dance.

"I can't believe we're going to this thing," I call out from the bathroom as I try to apply on make-up. I run a black pencil eyeliner on my waterline hoping not to poke myself in the eye. How do girls do this everyday?

I didn't want to wear any make-up but my mother and Britney insisted I had to. My mother also wanted me to wear my hair up, but I vetoed her choice and decided to wear my hair down. I flat ironed it pin straight and put a white flower hair clip in it. I actually like how my hair looks.

"I don't know. I'm kind of excited. At least it's a great reason to put on this hot dress." Britney says, coming in to show me her short, strapless satin green dress that hugs her body in all the right places.

"Wow, you look beautiful."

"Me?! Look at you. Court is going to go crazy when he sees you."

I smile. All I'm hoping for is he doesn't freak out when I tell him about Nash.

"Girls, your dates are here," my mother says, walking into my room. The moment she sees me her eyes become glassy. I know any minute she's going to release the tears she's trying to hold back. "Oh my God Emma, you look beautiful. Both of you look gorgeous!" I do feel pretty in my black ballerina styled dress. I'm not used to seeing myself like this.

"Thank yooouu…." My mother grabs me in her arms and hugs me tight. "Mom you're hurting me."

"I'm sorry. Its just, honey you don't know how proud I am of you."

"Because I'm going to a school dance?" I ask confused.

"No, because of the girl you've become." Tears begin to stream down her face. "I'm so happy you're my daughter. Always know how much I love you, and I would do anything for you." I don't understand why she's crying and saying all of this, but it's nice to feel this close to her. I give her another hug.

I look over at Britney, who is drying her eyes. I can't believe we made her tear up. She hardly ever sheds a tear, unless it's over a boy.

"Okay, no more of this. The boys are downstairs waiting for you." We follow her out of my room. I can't believe how hard my heart is beating.

At the bottom of my steps are Sam and Court. Sam looks so handsome in his black button down shirt and black pants with a white tie. When I spot his sneakers I can't help but smile, and then immediately become jealous. I wish I were wearing my Converses instead of these heels that are pinching my toes. No really, how do women handle this torture?

I look over at Court and feel my heart stop. He looks amazing in his light blue button down shirt and black dress pants. His eyes light up when he sees me, and a big smile spreads across his face showing off his perfect white teeth.

"You look beautiful," he says, when I reach his side.

"Thank you. You don't look so bad yourself."

"Thank you. Here, this is for you." He gives me a white orchid corsage.

"It's beautiful." He puts it on my wrist and then allows my mother to take a closer look at it.

"Court, it's beautiful! I'm telling you Emma, you are a very lucky girl to have him in your life," my mother says gushing over it. After tonight, I'm going to have to tell her the truth about everything.

My father walks in and immediately takes a step back when he sees me. "My baby girl," he says, sounding like his voice is going to crack any second. Oh God, I hope he doesn't start crying too. "You look…you look beautiful." A smile comes across his face. "But then again you always look beautiful."

It's exactly what I need to hear. He gives me a tight hug, and for a minute I wish I were still his little girl getting ready to watch a football game with him.

"Okay, picture time." My mother announces. She makes us pose in 100 different positions as she snaps away.

I quickly notice every time Court puts his arm around me, Sam suspiciously stares at us. I guess Nash put him on spy patrol, even though he said he wouldn't. Britney rolls her eyes as she notices this too. She whispers in his ear, which makes him deny whatever she's accusing him of.

"So you're ready to have fun?" Court asks, opening the car door.

I nod and smile, but inside my nerves are attacking my stomach.

The school gym is all dressed up in our school colors. Blue and white balloons and streamers decorate the ceiling. The middle of the gym is been assigned to be the dance floor. Surrounding the dance floor are round tables with plastic blue tablecloths adorning them and in the middle of each table lay little silver sparkly weights with blue and white balloons tied to them. It all actually looks tacky and pretty at the same time.

As soon as people notice we have entered the gym, everyone begins to cheer Court's name. He scored 18 points at the game today, and the last touchdown happened to be the one that won the game.

I take a step back to allow him the space to enjoy his spotlight, but he quickly grabs my hand and pulls me forward making my whole body turn red. I'm not a fan of this much attention.

"Wow, it's like we're with a celebrity," Britney says, as we continue to walk to our table, which is right by the dance floor.

"Everyone really does love you at this school," Sam says, looking as uncomfortable as I am.

"They just like my football skills," Court explains, pulling my chair out for me. "But there's only one person I like," he whispers in my ear, before I can sit down, making every hair on my arm rise. I smile, but it quickly vanishes when I spot Sam glaring at us again. His phone vibrates right on cue and Sam turns to text back. He's been texting non-stop since we left my house.

Court sits next to me and drapes his arm around the back of my chair. I move forward afraid if he touches me, Sam will start texting Nash again. I hate feeling so self-conscious.

"Are you okay?" Court asks sitting up to be closer to me.

"Yeah, just trying to take this all in."

"I'm glad you came. There's no other person I would want here with me." I wish he wouldn't look at me with those eyes, which somehow still manages to melt my heart.

I know I sound like an immature brat who doesn't know what she wants. But I do know who I want, and it's Nash. This doesn't mean I still don't have feelings for Court. The truth is, there will always be a piece of my heart that belongs to him.

The whole table shakes as Sam's phone vibrates again. Just before he can pick it up Britney snatches it and begins to text away. I let out a small laugh; I know she's letting Nash have it.

"Lets go dance!" Britney grabs Sam's hand and pulls him onto the dance floor before he can object.

"What was that all about?" Court asks, turning his body to watch Britney and Sam argue.

"I have no idea."

"Well I'm glad they left us alone," Court says taking hold of my hand resting on the table.

Even though Sam is no longer near us, I still feel self-conscience about Court touching me. It's as if Nash is watching me. I pull my hand out of his and stand up. "Hey, let's go dance," I say.

"What?"

"We came here to dance so let's dance."

"Okay, let's do this." Court smiles, leading me to the dance floor.

The latest pop song is blaring out of the speakers as I move my hips from side to side. In my mind I think I'm dancing like one of those girls from any of the Step Up movies, but I can't get my body to pop and lock like they do.

Court and I stay out on the dance floor song after song. We both laugh at his dancing skills. He might have moves on the football field, but when it comes to the dance floor he has none. He's actually making my dance skills look good. I can't believe I'm having this much fun at school dance.

Sam seems to be calmer after arguing with Britney. He doesn't even glance my way. He's too busy staring at Britney with loving eyes. It's good to know that she is with someone who truly loves her. This time last year she was crying over one boy while hooking up with two others. How things have changed.

Two hours after arriving, our vice principal, Mr. Cruz, stops our dancing to announce the homecoming king and queen. Of course everyone picked the two most popular students at Cypress Oak High. They stand up on stage pretending they had no idea they were going to win. Whatever! These people make me sick and remind me of why I can't stand school functions.

They walk off the stage and begin to dance to the first slow song of the night. We all stand around looking at the beautiful couple with their plastic crowns on their heads. I gaze over at Court and know he's going to be wearing that crown next year. I just hope we have some form of friendship when that time comes.

Mr. Cruz once again speaks into the microphone and asks everyone to join the king and queen on the dance floor. Court takes my hand and leads me to the middle of the floor right next to the royal couple.

He locks his arms around my waist forcing me to wrap my arms around his neck. I quickly scan the room for Sam and find him making out with Britney on the other side of the gym, which makes me feel safe to dance this close to Court.

"Are you having fun?" he asks, gazing into my eyes.

"I really am." But guilt is starting to bear down on me. I shouldn't be having this much fun without Nash.

"Well if you think this place is fun, wait 'til the after party at Adam's house."

I knew this moment was going to come sooner or later, I just wish it would come up a lot later. "I'm not going to the after party." I whisper, no longer able to look into his eyes.

"I know you don't like my friends but I promise…."

"No, that's not it."

"Then what is it? I already asked your parents if you could stay out and they both said yes."

"I know. It's just…." I finally look up to meet his eyes. A tight ball forms in my throat squeezing it so hard it hurts. Why can't this be easy?

"It's just what? Look if you don't wanna go to Adam's then we won't. We'll do something else. I don't want this night to end."

His words make the knot in my throat not only choke, but also burn my vocal chords. "I can't...I can't go with you after the dance, because...I'm already meeting someone else," I manage to utter slowly.

He drops his arms limply at his sides. "What? Who are you meeting?"

I unwrap my arms from his neck and stare down at the floor as the knot that's formed in my throat now forms in my stomach. *Come on Emma you can do this. You owe him the truth.* "Nash."

"What?" Court's eyes fly open. "You're meeting Nash?"

"Yes."

"Why?"

"We're back together. I wanted to tell you before but...."

"I can't believe you," Court says, with disgust in his voice. His eyes turn dark. He drops his head, turns around, and storms out of the dance. The tears I tried so hard to keep back now spill out. I need him to understand.

I run past the students grinding to the new song playing. I run past all the tables, which have way too many plastic cups on them. I open the gym doors and find Court pacing back and forth in the hallway.

"Court, please let me explain."

"Explain what? That he used you to hurt me, and now you're back with him like it didn't happen. What the hell is wrong with you? How could you go back with him?"

"It's not that simple. He's sorry. He admitted he made a mistake. I have to try to see if...."

"I don't wanna hear this. I knew this was going to fucking happen. I knew if I let you back in my life again, you would crush me once more." Rage takes over his whole body and with pure anger he says, "The biggest mistake I've ever made is sleeping with you."

"Please don't say that."

"Well it's the truth. I'm such an idiot. But know this right now, when Nash hurts you again, and trust me he will do it, don't expect me to be there to pick up the pieces. I'm done with you. I'm done being part of your selfish games. I no longer want to know you." He turns around and exits out to the parking lot.

My tears fall faster, burning my skin. I can't believe I hurt him like this again. I need to make him understand. I can't let our friendship end like this.

15
The Only One

I know I told Emma that I wouldn't ask Sam to watch over her, but I couldn't help asking him to do it. I've been texting him since he told me he was on his way to pick up the girls. He keeps telling me everything is cool and I don't have anything to worry about, but I have this gut feeling Court doesn't just think of Emma as a friend. I know he'll try to use tonight to get her back.

Leo and Jen are helping me set up for my private after party with Emma. Leo is starting to get annoyed that I keep stopping to send Sam a message. "Will you stop texting him," he says plugging in the last set of lights.

"I know! This is the last time." I grab my phone and quickly text Sam, **"What's going on now?"**

Seconds later my phone beeps. I look at it with my heart beating fast. I'm not sure what I want to see or don't want to see. **"Leave Sam alone! Leave us all alone! BTW this is Britney if u hadn't guessed**." Damn it. Why does she always have to stick her nose where it doesn't belong? I guess I'm really done texting Sam.

Thirty minutes later, I thank Leo and Jen for all their help and jump in my truck. I still have one more hour until I have to meet up with Emma. I can drive around for a while, but I already know all I'm going to do is drive in circles around Cypress Oak High School.

I could always go to the Free Bird Café and hang out with Mila, but she's not too happy with me for having her cover another one of my shifts. This sucks! I'm just going to go to the school and wait outside in the parking lot. It's only an hour. I can do this.

I park my truck facing the gym doors and roll my window down to listen to the horrible music coming from inside. I wish I could see what's going on in there. It's driving me crazy. I hate thinking Emma is inside having a good time with that douche bag.

The music stops and a muffled voice make an announcement followed by cheers. I wonder if she is standing next to Court smiling and cheering.

Seconds after the announcement, slow music begins to play and my heart palpitates with anger. I close my eyes and picture Court holding Emma in his arms. I picture him leaning in to kiss her. Each vision sears more rage into my veins. I can't take this anymore.

I jump out of my truck and storm over to the metal doors. I need to get her right now, before Court tries anything. I grasp the cold handle, and right before I open the door I freeze. I can't do this; Emma would never forgive me for ruining her night.

The slow song ends, and some poppy crap starts to play. I take a deep breath and walk back to my truck. I need to trust Emma. She's not Angie. I can trust her.

Instead of sitting in my truck, I jump on the hood and watch the grey metal doors. Suddenly, the doors fly open and Court steps out looking furious. I jump off my truck just in time to catch his dark eyes glaring my way. I guess he found out about Emma and me.

Happiness begins to fill my heart again. Court walks toward me as if he's going to hit me. I'm ready. I can take him. My body freezes when I catch a glimpse of Emma running out with tears in her eyes. I stumble backwards, not because I'm scared of Court, but because she looks so beautiful. It knocks the wind out of me.

"Court!" She screams out.

He stops to look her way and then turns to face me again. He snaps with a thick voice, "You're not worth it. She's all yours. Break her heart if you want, I don't care anymore. As far as I know, you two deserve each other." I'm not sure whether to thank him, or punch him in the face.

He walks past me and disappears into the pitch-black parking lot. I gaze over at Emma who's now crying harder. Her whole frame trembles. I walk over to her as fast as I can and let her fall into my arms.

"I didn't wanna hurt him like this," she cries.

"I know." I pull her in tighter. I hate that she's crying over that asshole, but at the same time I'm happy she's finally in my arms and out of his forever.

"Emma, are you okay?" Britney asks, walking out the door with Sam behind her. Why does she always have to appear to ruin a moment?

"No. Court found out that I'm back with Nash. He's furious," Emma answers, trying to dry her never-ending tears.

"How did he find out?" Britney asks, eyeing me suspiciously. *Let me guess, she thinks I had something to do with it.* "You couldn't let them enjoy this night. You had to come here to ruin everything." *I was right. She thinks it's all my fault.*

"It wasn't him! I told him. Court wanted me to go to the after party with him. I had to tell him why I couldn't go. He's so mad at me. The last time I saw him this mad, was the last time he found out I was seeing Nash."

"He'll get over it," I let slip out.

Britney glares my way before she blurts out, "I'm sure you're enjoying every minute of his pain right now."

"I didn't mean it like that."

"I'm sure you didn't," Britney sarcastically states with a tight lip smile.

"Britney stop! Please just stop. Look, I need to get out of here. Do you guys need a ride?" Emma asks, looking defeated.

"No. I have my car," Sam speaks up. Britney and Emma both look at him confused. "I had Court pick me up here. I kinda figured once he knew the truth, Britney and me would have to find a way home."

"Court didn't ask you why you had him meet you here?" Britney asks still looking puzzled.

"I told him I wanted to be alone with you after the dance." Sam leans in and gives her a kiss on the lips, calming the lioness down.

"You ready to get out of here?" I ask Emma still holding her hand.

"Yeah." She walks over and gives Britney and Sam a hug goodbye.

They both start walking back to the dance, but not before Britney makes sure to give me an evil glare. I know that's her way of warning me not to do anything to hurt her best friend. As much as I can't stand her, I like that she's such a good friend to Emma, and an even better girlfriend to Sam.

I walk Emma to my truck and open the door for her. She hops in and gives me a half smile before I close the door. I run to the driver's side hoping she likes what I have in store for her. At least I hope it cheers her up and takes her mind off that idiot.

* * *

I wish I could get rid of the pain piercing my heart at this moment. I should have told Court about Nash when he asked me to homecoming, just like I now should tell Nash the truth about Court. But what if Nash reacts the same way Court did? I'm so scared of losing him too.

That stupid knot is making its comeback in my throat. Tears reappear in the corners of my eyes. Why can't I be one of those girls who don't cry? Do those girls even exist?

Nash looks over at me and I can see his disappointment in my sadness. I try to smile again and ask, "Where are we going?"

"It's a surprise. Look, I know you've had a tough night, and if you prefer to go home it's…."

"What? No. I'll be okay. I've waited all night to see you. All I wanna do now is spend some time with you." Nash's face lights up.

I recognize the road as we enter Monticello. "Are we going to Leo's?"

"Yeah."

"Why? Is he having a party?"

149

"You can say that." I can't help but feel disappointed. I was hoping to spend some time alone with Nash.

As we drive up Leo's dirt road, I notice the house is dark and Leo's car is not in the driveway. Ohmigod, we have the house to ourselves. What if Nash wants to go back where we left off right before we broke up?

We were supposed to sleep together the day I found out the truth about our relationship. I can't have sex with Nash yet. My insides tangle with anxiety, I'm going to have to tell him the truth tonight.

Nash parks the truck, hops out, and runs to my side to open my door. He gives me his hand, which is as clammy as mine, and helps me out. The smell of burning wood tickles my nose. Maybe there is a party, but I don't hear anyone. He leads me towards the back of the house.

I take each nervous step excited to see what is waiting for me. We turn the corner, and I feel my heart jump out of my chest when I see what Nash has set up for me.

All the lights Leo had set up for Leo-stock are lit up making it look like a white light wonderland. In the middle of the yard is a fire pit with the most perfect fire. On the side is a table with a white tablecloth on it and red roses petals in a shape of a heart. In the middle of the heart is a bottle of ginger ale and two champagne glasses. I can't believe he did all this for me. Even though there's a cool breeze, my body feels warm with exultation.

I jump when I hear Nash turn on the music. Yellowcard's song *Sing for Me* begins to play.

"I wanted us to have our own homecoming dance. Can I have this dance?" Nash asks, taking my hand.

"Of course." His arms slip around my waist as I automatically put my arms around his neck. All the sorrow I was feeling before is gone. Nash is the one person who can always make me forget the pain in my heart. "This is all so beautiful."

"You're the one who's beautiful."

"It's the dress, it makes me look good."

"The dress does look amazing, but it's only because of the girl that's in it," he says holding me tighter.

I can't stop my whole body from blushing. I still can't believe Nash did all of this for me. This is all so wildly romantic.

"Your heart is beating so fast," I say, feeling it beat against my chest.

"You do that to me."

He brings his face closer to mine and gently strokes my cheek with his. The smell of his cologne teases all of my senses. I lift my head up just in time to meet his sweet lips with mine. Nash is everything I've always wanted, and when I lost him I thought I would never be able to heal. Now standing here with him, I know I wouldn't have. I'm in love with him.

The song ends, but we stay in each other's arms as if we are glued together. I'm so happy I decided to meet him after the dance. There's no other place I'd rather be.

"You thirsty?" He asks, taking my hand and walking me towards the table.

"Yes. I still can't believe you did all of this."

"Well I didn't do it alone. Leo and Jen helped me."

"Where are they?"

"They went away for the night." My heart races again knowing they are not coming back. It must be obvious because Nash immediately says, "Nothing is going to happen tonight that you don't want to happen."

"I know. I mean…It's just that right before we broke up, we were going to…you know." *Why can't I speak like a normal person?*

"I know. Emma, I don't wanna go back to where we left off. I wanna start all over with you. I wanna show you what a good boyfriend I can be, and earn your trust before anything else can happen." I lean in and kiss him once more. He's already proving to be an amazing boyfriend.

We spend the rest of the night talking, dancing, but mostly kissing. His kisses are passionate and firm making every essence of my body yearn for more. Now I know what writers are talking about when they describe the perfect kiss.

Two and half hours later, it's Nash who realizes it's time to get me home. "We better get going."

"And here I thought you were going to try to get me to spend the night," I tease.

"I would love to have you spend the night with me, but I remember the last time that happened. I don't need your parents hating me more than I think they already do," he chuckles.

I wrap my arms around him and give him a tight hug. It's funny how a few hours ago I was crying my eyes out, and now I can't stop smiling. Tonight was just right. Hopefully tomorrow won't be as hard as I think it will be. I look at the clock in Nash's truck and realize it's already tomorrow. Happy Birthday Jason.

I open my eyes with the same smile I had last night when I fell asleep. I sit up in bed and a pain takes over my heart. It's hard to believe Jason is no longer here to celebrate his birthday. I remember last year, we all skipped school and drove to New York City to celebrate.

We had an awesome time walking around Greenwich Village and dreaming of one day living there. Jason did not drink that day, and I remember thinking how much I love him, just like I love Britney.

I miss him so much. He really was a great friend. A part of me wishes I never crossed the line between friendship and boyfriend. Then maybe that night I wouldn't have pushed him away and he would still be here. Tears fall from my eyes, as the memories build.

"Emma?" My mom says, slightly opening my bedroom door.

I quickly dry my eyes. "Yeah?"

"I was just coming to see how last night went." She walks into my room smiling, but also looks tired. I wonder if she stayed up waiting for me.

"It was okay."

"It was okay? Come on Emma, I want to know everything."

"Mom, can we talk about this later?"

She purses her lips, "Fine. But when you come downstairs, I want to know everything."

"Fine." I watch her walk out of my room before I collapse back onto my bed. How am I going to tell my mother that once again I broke Court's heart, and I think this time he might not forgive me. This really sucks.

Right before I head downstairs, I receive a text from Nash letting me know he's on his way to pick me up. I quickly text him back to meet me at the bottom of my street. I'm not ready to let my parents know I'm back with him just yet. At least not until I let them know my fake relationship with Court is over.

I walk into the kitchen and notice my parents are back to ignoring each other. My dad is reading his newspaper with anger spread across his face, while my mother sits next to him sipping her coffee looking out to nowhere. No wonder she looks so tired.

I wish whatever is going on between them would already stop. Why can't they go back to being my happy parents, who talk about world issues, the economy, or whatever movie they are going to watch?

"Good morning," I say, startling them.

"Good morning," my father mumbles.

"Oh good, you're here. Okay, come sit next to me and tell me everything," My mother says tapping the chair next to her.

"There's not much to tell. We got there, we danced, and then we left."

"Oh come on Emma! Tell me about the decorations."

"They were blue and white balloons and streamers."

"Emma, I swear you're no fun when it comes to this," my mother huffs, slamming her coffee cup on the table. I can't believe she's getting this upset over not getting all the details.

"Mom, I'm sorry. It's just I don't know what to tell you. It was a school dance. You know."

"No, I don't know. I never got to go to one." She pushes her seat from the table and takes her mug to the kitchen sink.

"Here we go again. I swear Susan, it's time to get over your high school years," my father says rolling his eyes.

"Oh that's easy for you to say. You had a great time in high school," My mother answers him, looking hurt.

"Fine. Go cry about how you never got to go to a school dance with Peter Dobberson." My father replies angrily, before he stands up and storms out of the kitchen.

"What was that about?" I ask my mother, who is now trying to wash the navy blue color off her mug.

"Nothing.

"Mom!?"

She crosses her arms under her chest. "Your dad found out about my crush on Peter."

Now I understand why he's been so mad. But her crush on Mr. Dobberson was so long ago, why would it bother him now? "Doesn't he realize it was a crush you had in high school?"

"Yes, he's more mad at the fact that I kept it a secret. He's funny that way. Well, I have papers to correct. What are you up to today?" She asks.

"I'm going to go hang out with Britney." I don't want to remind her it's Jason's birthday. I'm afraid she'll keep me from going to the cemetery.

"Okay, have fun." She walks out looking broken.

I guess it doesn't matter how old a secret is, it still stings when the truth comes out. I just hope my father gets over this quickly.

16
<u>Heavy Heart</u>

To be completely honest, it does bother me to have to wait for Emma at the bottom of her street. It's close enough where it's a quick walk for her and far enough where her parents can't see me.

I wish things were different and her mom would want her to be with me instead of Court. I guess I shouldn't complain, since my mom doesn't approve of this relationship either.

Emma texts me to let me know she's on her way out. I'm not sure how I feel about going to a cemetery with her. The last time I went to one was when Ben was buried. I haven't gone back since that day. I don't like to think about his body being under all the dirt. It makes me feel claustrophobic.

"Hey," Emma says, appearing at the passenger side window.

"Hey."

She opens the door, jumps in, and leans over to give me a delicious kiss setting off sparks inside me. I love having her this close again.

"You ready?" I ask.

"Yeah."

"How are you doing with everything?"

"It's been a tough morning dealing with Jason not being here for his birthday. I don't know if it will ever feel okay," She says on the verge of tears.

"I know how you feel. Ben's birthday is May 28th and the anniversary of his death is June 12th. It was the hardest two weeks I've been through in a long time. It was as if he had died all over again. I'm not looking forward to the next anniversary."

"Wow, that must've been so hard. How old would he have been?"

"20." My heart aches talking about it, but at the same time, it's good to share all this with her. After Ben died, my family stopped talking about him. They didn't even discuss the good memories. It's as if they say his name out loud, we will all fall apart.

It wasn't until I met Emma that I became comfortable talking about Ben again. I think it's one of the biggest reasons I fell in love with her. She made it easy to talk about him.

We turn into the cemetery and I immediately have trouble breathing. Emma must sense my discomfort, because she reaches her hand out and wraps it around mine. "If you don't wanna go with me, you can wait in the truck. It's okay." She smiles making it easier to inhale and exhale again. I have to get over my discomfort and be there for her.

"No. I wanna go with you."

We both get out of my truck and head towards Jason's headstone. The cold wind sends a chill straight into my bones. Rows and rows of headstones line the grounds. It's so strange to think there are bodies under each one of them.

I remember, when I was a kid, every time we drove past a cemetery, I would close my eyes in fear that the dead bodies would rise from their graves and chase after me. It was all Ben's fault; he had me watch Dawn of the Dead with him when I was only six years old. It scared the shit out of me. Years later, I hate to admit a part of me still fears the same thing.

When we get to Jason's headstone, I notice fresh flowers have been placed on his grave. "Someone was already here," I say holding her hand tightly.

"Yeah, it was his dad."

"How'd you know?"

"It's the same kind of flowers he had set up for the funeral. White carnations were Jason's favorite, because they could turn any color you want, including black." Emma starts laughing while she remembers. "He would dye white carnations black all the time, and place them all over his house, pissing off his stepmother. He really loved to irk her."

"It sounds like I would've liked him."

"Most definitely. He was the funniest, most caring, loving friend anyone could have." She sits by his headstone, smiles, and begins talking to him, "Happy Birthday. I'm sure where ever you are you're celebrating. I'm glad to see your father came to see you. I know it must have warmed your heart to see he remembered."

She turns around and gives me one of her amazing smiles, and then turns back to Jason's headstone. "Anyway, Jason I would like you to meet Nash. Yes this the famous Nash. The one I cried about." It breaks my heart to hear her say those words. I never want to make her cry again. "But now things are good between us and I'm happy again. Jason, I'm sorry for not being a good friend for you towards the end. I would do anything to take back all I said to you the night before...."

I put my hand on her shoulder. I know she blames herself for Jason's death. I know I can't change it, but I hope I can soothe her pain by letting her know I'm here for her. I sit right next to her fighting the uneasiness is sitting in the pit of my stomach.

"I miss him so much," she begins to sob.

"I know."

"I hate this. I wish there was something I could do to bring him back."

Tears travel down her cheeks. I pull her close to me and hold her as she weeps in my arms. I wipe tears off her soft skin. "What was Jason like?"

"What?"

"Tell me about Jason." I know when I talk about Ben with her I feel better; I'm hoping I can do the same for her.

"He was funny. I mean really funny. He always had to make you laugh no matter how mad you were at him." Her eyes light up when she speaks about him. "He was the type of person you could tell your deepest secrets to, knowing he would never tell a soul. He was my best friend."

I don't know why, but her love for him makes me love her even more. She makes me wish I would have been able to meet Jason.

"Is Ben's grave nearby?" She asks taking me by surprise.

"No. He's buried up in Michigan. It was my grandparent's idea."

"That must be hard, not being able to go there."

"I guess. I try not to think about it." I don't want to let her know how uncomfortable I am at cemeteries.

"Well if you ever want me to take the trip with you to Michigan, I'll be happy to go." I nod draping my arms around her shoulders. I know the day I do decide to visit my brother's grave the only person I will want by my side is Emma.

* * *

Going to see Jason is exactly what I needed. After, Nash and me head to get something to eat at the Blue Moon Diner in Monticello. We both sit in the booth emotionally exhausted. I think bringing Nash with me got him thinking about Ben. Maybe I shouldn't have asked him to come with me.

"Are you okay?" I ask playing with the straw in my glass.

He gives me a partial grin and says, "Yeah, just thinking about life."

"And Ben?"

"Yeah. I miss him a lot. Every time something wonderful happens in my life I want to share it with him." He grabs both of my hands. "I wish I could've introduced him to you."

"Do you think he would've liked me?"

"Are you kidding me? He would've loved you. How about Jason? You think he would've liked me?"

"Of course. And if you would've let him take your bike for a spin he would've became your number one fan." Nash starts to laugh as a warm glow comes back into his eyes.

"Thank you."

"For what?"

"For giving me the opportunity to be here with you. I was so scared you were never going to give me another chance."

I smile and lean in to give him a kiss on his cheek. I'm the one who's thankful he did not give up on me.

We eat the rest of our meal laughing, sharing more stories about Jason and Ben. I tell him about the time Jason and me decided to become independent documentarians after watching the movie Reality Bites, and did video journals on our friends. Our passion only lasted a week, before Jason decided he rather write music, even though he did not know how to read one note.

Nash tells me about the time Ben decided to go house to house collecting money by pretending it was for animals in shelters. When his mother found out, she made him go back to each house and return the money.

After our meal, we head to Main Street and go into different stores. We look at vintage concert posters in one store, and try on different sunglasses in another.

Nash takes me to Ever Inked and introduces me to the owner Dan. They both talk about the business and Nash's future there. I sit there and listen to every word in full bliss. I love seeing how his golden green eyes glow with excitement when he discusses his apprenticeship.

Before I know it, our day is over, and we are sitting in Nash's truck heading back to my house. "I had a really good time today," Nash says, taking his eyes off the road, to quickly gaze into my eyes.

"Yeah me too."

"So, am I dropping you off at the top of your street, or the bottom?"

"Neither. Drop me off in front."

"Are you sure?"

"Yes." I say feeling bubbles of elation in my stomach. "I'm with you and it's time my parents learn to deal with it." A bigger smile comes across his face.

I'm not making the same mistake I did the first time with Nash. This time, I'm going to be honest with my parents. I know at first they won't be thrilled, but I'm sure after a while they will learn to accept him. They really don't have a choice.

We pull up in front of my house, where I can see the living room lights shining through the windows. I stare at my house waiting to see if either of my parents look out the window, but neither one of them does.

I turn around to face Nash who is staring at me. I scoot closer to him. He places his warm hand on my cold cheek, and softly strokes my face with the back of his fingers. His face draws nearer to mine. It doesn't matter how many times he's kissed me, every time he goes to kiss me again it makes my heart races. His eyes close and right before our lips meet he whispers, "Don't go in yet." Sending little sensations across my lips.

I nod.

Our lips connect and we begin to kiss me. Our tongues dance and intertwine in each other's mouth, sending me into pure ecstasy. His hands navigate up and down my back, making every part of me shiver with excitement.

This is our first real make-out session since getting back together, and the way my body is reacting is scaring me. I want him to touch me all over. I want him to make me his.

Before I know it, I sit on top of him with the steering wheel digging into my back. I find my hands wandering all over his chest, as I aggressively kiss him, forgetting my parents are only a few feet away, and any minute could look out the window and see us. His lips land on my neck as his warm hands begin to go up my shirt, sending tiny shock waves up and down my spine. A loud voice starts to scream in my head. I try to ignore it but it just screams louder until I screech to a halt.

"We can't do this here," I say climbing off him.

"We could always drive down to the end of the street."

I start laughing. "Call me when you get home."

Nash gives a painful grunt before smiling. "Okay. I love you."

"I Love you too." I jump out of his truck, happy we stopped before anything else could happen. The loud voice kept reminding me nothing can happen between us until I tell him about Court. Damn, I hate the stupid voice inside my head.

A shooting star skates across the black sky, which makes me think it's Jason partying on his birthday. The corners of my mouth go up so high it actually starts to hurt. I open the front door and immediately feel my smile dissolve when the sounds of my parents fighting reach my ears. My heart pounds hard as I slowly make my way to the kitchen, where they once again have chosen to be their place of war.

"What about me? Your choices affect me too. Don't you get it?" My father yells at my mother, who is sitting at the kitchen table with her head buried in her hands.

"What choices?" I ask interrupting them.

My father whips his head around and I notice his brown eyes are as swollen as my mother's. Why is he crying? I've never seen him cry before, not even when my grandfather died.

"It's nothing that concerns you," My mother says, drying her eyes with the back of her hand.

"That's right, let's keep more people in the dark," My father sternly says.

"Michael, this does not concern her!" My mother almost screams.

"It will sooner or later." He walks out of the kitchen without even looking at me. What does he mean it will concern me sooner or later? Are my parents breaking up?

That nasty evil lump reappears in my throat, making it hard to swallow. I stand there flipping through my vocabulary to find the perfect words, which might make her tell me what's going on.

"So, where have you been? Did Court meet up with Britney and you?"

"What was Dad talking about? Is he still mad about your crush on Mr. Dobberson?"

"What? No. It's something between your father and I."

"But Dad said it would affect m…."

"Enough! I said it's nothing." She stands up and storms out of the kitchen. I wish somebody in this family would tell me what's going on, because I'm starting to get scared now.

17
Throwing Stones

I'm still on a high from my date with Emma, and not in the mood to go home yet. After, spending the day talking about Ben, I know exactly who I need to go see.

"Hey, this is a good surprise," Roxy says opening her door. Ryder sits on her right hip with a huge Kool Aid smile. He has the same sparkling blue eyes Roxy does.

"Are you busy?"

"Not at all. Come in."

"I can't believe how big he's gotten," I say, grabbing his tiny hand and making him laugh. I always wished Ryder had been Ben's son. It would have been nice to have someone to carry on his image.

"I know. He turned nine months old just yesterday."

"Nash! How are you?" Roxy's mom says walking into the living room. I lean over to give her a hug hello.

"I'm good. How are you Ms. Becker?"

"Pretty good. How's your mom? It's been too long since I've seen her."

"She's okay. Working hard all the time."

"Well it's tough being a single mother," she says walking towards Roxy.

Ms. Becker is in her forties but looks like she's still in her late twenties. She has the same platinum blond hair as Roxy and the bright blue eyes seem to run in the family. When I first met her I instantly fell in love with her. I used to tell Roxy I was going to marry her mother and be her stepdad. She would always punch me and throw a hissy fit. To this day, I still feel like the twelve-year-old boy with a huge crush when I'm around her.

"Do you want me to take him?" She asks Roxy.

"Yes, please." Ms. Becker puts her arms out and Ryder jumps into them. "Thanks mom."

"No problem. It was nice seeing you again Nash. Please tell your mother I said hello."

"I will," I say, watching her walk out of the small living room. "Your mom is great."

"Yeah, she is. I couldn't have handled the last two years without her." Roxy takes a black elastic off her wrist and puts her hair up in a messy bun as she sits pretzel legs on her black leather couch. "So what's up? I know you didn't just stop by to say hi."

I take a seat next to her. "You're right. I went to the cemetery with Emma today, and it got me thinking about Ben. Do you ever wish he had been buried closer?"

She starts to play with the undone hem of her green T-shirt. "I guess. I mean I know his body is up in Michigan, but my memories of him are in here." She points to her head and then points to her heart as she says, "And in here." Her eyes turn glassy. I know Roxy is going to do everything she can to hold back those tears.

"I guess you're right."

"So, how are things with Emma?" She quickly wipes her eyes.

"Really good."

"What about Court? How are you dealing with him?"

"I'm not sure they're still friends. He was really mad when he found out we were back together."

She shakes her head in disappointment. "And what if they work things out? Can you be with Emma if Court is in her life?"

"I'll deal with it." Why does she always have to doubt us? "Look, I know Court is your choice for her. I mean why wouldn't he be? He's the good guy and I'm the bad boy who doesn't...."

"That's where you're wrong Nash. You are not the bad boy. You've made mistakes, but that doesn't make you the bad one. You're actually the good one, and I don't want you to get hurt."

"I'm not gonna get hurt. What Emma and I have is real, and her friendship with Court is not going to ruin it."

"I sure hope so," she says, giving me a fretful look.

* * *

After having to live in a house full of thick hostile air I'm happy to be heading back to school, but I'm also nervous. I have no idea what's going to happen when I see Court. I know I should talk to him and see if I can save our friendship.

I tried texting him all weekend long, but he never answered me. When I spoke to Britney, she told me Court went back to the dance after I left, and decided to hang out with his friends. She said Christy was all over him, which I knew was going to happen.

"So how was your weekend?" Britney asks, meeting me at my locker.

"Good. I went to the cemetery for Jason's birthday."

"Why didn't you tell me you were going? I would've gone with you."

"Sorry. I went with Nash."

Anger enters her eyes as she crinkles her nose. "Of course you did."

"What's that supposed to mean?"

"It's just, I still don't get why you would choose him over Court again. Court is so good to you...."

"Because I am not in love with Court."

"But you never really gave him a chance. You might have fallen in love with him."

"Britney, can't you see if I went out with Court it would be the same thing I did with Jason. I would only be going out with him to keep him in my life. Besides when your heart belongs to someone else you can't force it to fall for anyone else."

"I guess you're right."

"Actually, your brother was right."

"Huh?" She looks confused.

"Johnny is who said that, and he was so right."

"I'm scared of you getting hurt again." Britney leans against the locker as if she's in pain.

"Me too, but I can't let that fear control me." I walk away wishing those words applied to everything in my life. Right now, I'm letting my fear control me from seeing Court.

I've been doing a great job avoiding Court. Actually it hasn't been hard, since he doesn't seems to be around. Neither Britney nor I have seen or heard his voice all day. This doesn't stop my stomach from spinning as I approach my last class. There's no way to avoid him in here. I think I'm going to be sick.

I enter the classroom and relief enters my body when I see his empty seat. Maybe he isn't here. But then again Christy is not here either and they can both walk in together any minute.

The hard cold uncomfortable desk holds me in place as my insides freeze when Court's laughter from outside of the room travels inside. He laughs again; maybe this is a good thing. His light mood might make it easier to speak to him. He might not be mad at me anymore.

Court steps inside with Christie by his side. I knew this was going to happen. Christy is like his dog. As soon as he gives her some attention she comes running with her tail wagging.

He heads straight to his seat and sits down without even glancing my way. Okay, so this is going to be a lot harder than I thought.

Mrs. Kennel talks for thirty minutes about the Merchant of Venice. I hardly listen to one word she says. I'm too busy staring at the back of Court's head, which only turns to glance over at Christy. Damn him!

Then just as I think it can't get any worse, Mrs. Kennel announces, "Now for the last fifteen minutes of class I'm going to ask you to get into your assigned reading groups to discuss the book your group has chosen."

Desks immediately begin to screech on the white tiled floor as my stomach churns with uneasiness. I slowly push my desk towards my group, which has decided to park themselves in front of the windows. Court quickly pulls Christy and Lilly's desk next to him. Okay, he wants to play this game.

I shove my desk up against his so we're right across from each other. This time he has no choice but to look at me. Wrong again. He turns his head slightly and starts to talk to Christy. She bats her evil blue eyes at him while she twirls her fake blond hair. She isn't fooling anyone with that hair. You can see her dark roots from a mile away. I can't take this anymore.

"Shouldn't we start talking about the book?" I finally say, after having to listen to Christy giggles like a hyena for the last five minutes.

"Okay, let's talk about the theme of Metamorphous," Court says looking down at his book.

I take a deep breathe and say, "Well I think a big theme of this book is the way people can make someone feel when they don't feel like part of the wor…."

"Yeah, no." Court interrupts me rolling his eyes. "I think it's something deeper than that."

Lilly speaks up and makes the same point I was just trying to make, and of course Court thinks it brilliant. I want to reach over and make him look at me in the eyes. I sit across from him feeling rejected.

For the next ten minutes Court shoots down whatever I try to say without ever looking up at me, which is really starting to irritate me. Christy enjoys every minute of it.

The bell finally rings just as my body fills with rage. Why is he acting like such a baby? I wonder if he's ever going to stop being mad at me. All of a sudden the rage exits my body like a balloon deflating. I can't blame him for his hostile attitude towards me. It's going to take a lot to get him to forgive me. Even though, I don't owe him any legal debt, I might actually have to offer him a pound of flesh to forgive me.

He grabs his bag and then Christy's hand sending bullets into my heart. I know I have no right to be angry, but I can't help it. Why does he have to pick my archenemy to be with? They begin to walk out the door, and I know if I don't ask to speak him now I'll never will.

"Court!"

Everyone in the class, who hasn't left yet, turns around to face me. Maybe I shouldn't have yelled his name out.

"What?" He says, finally looking at me.

I slowly make my way over to him as everyone keeps staring at us. My legs feel like Jello. "Do you think we can talk?"

"I have nothing to say to you."

"Please?"

"He said he has nothing to say to you," Christy spits out with a wicked smile.

"Court, please. For just a minute," I beg as everyone still looks on.

Christy steps in between us and barks, "You really are stupid...."

"Fine, but not here," Court says interrupting her.

I follow him out of the room while Christy stands there with her arms folded under her chest looking disgusted. In a way I wish I could talk to her too and find out why we hate each other so much. I don't think that's ever going to happen.

Court walks beside me down the packed hallway without making a sound. Every muscle in his body is tight with fury. I'm starting to change my mind; maybe I don't really need to talk to him right this minute. Everyone in the hall whispers as we walk by them.

"Where are we going?" I ask, hoping he'll finally say something.

"In here," he says opening the door to a dark classroom. I enter the room scared to death for what's about to happen.

Court closes the door as people walking by try to get a peek inside. He turns on the light, and comes to stand in front of me without any emotion on his face. Maybe this won't be so bad. "Okay talk," he says.

"Okay, um…well first I want to say sor…."

"You know what Emma, I'm sick and tired of hearing the word sorry come out of your mouth. Just say what you have to tell me, so I can go and live my life without you."

"That's just it, why can't we talk and try to save our friendship?"

"When you chose to get back with that asshole you also chose to end our friendship," Court says running his finger through his hair as he walks to the other side of the room.

I follow him. "But why? Why can't you and I continue to be friends? I don't understand."

"You're gonna tell me Nash will be okay with us being friends?" He points to the door as if Nash was standing right outside.

"Yeah. He just wants me to be happy. And having you in my life makes me happy."

"Find someone else to make you happy, because I'm done being your friend," Court says making quotation marks around the word *friend*. "I told you Emma I wasn't going to play the fool again. You wanna be with Nash well then good for you. The both of you can be miserable together. You want me in your life, well that isn't gonna happen with him in it."

I choke up the tears that are trying desperately to escape my eyes. I'm done begging him to remain in my life. "You know what, you're right. Our friendship is over. You wanna drop me because I'm with Nash well then fine." I walk towards the door and right before I open it I turn around and say, "I don't need you. I didn't need you all those years you were way up on your high horse to know who I was, and I don't need you now. And to think I thought Jason had sent you my way to make me smile again. I should've known better. He wouldn't ever have sent the guy that used to make fun of him. I was an idiot for falling for your nice guy routine." I turn around and walk out the classroom before any of my tears have a chance to make their way down my face. I will never let him see me cry again.

It only takes seconds to regret everything I just said. I was so mad and I wanted him to hurt the same way he was hurting me. Losing Court for a second time is even more painful than the first.

18
No One Said It Would Be Easy

Emma called me crying and told me about her conversation with Court. I wish I could say I wasn't happy about his decision to not be in her life anymore, but I am. At the same time I feel like I owe him. If he hadn't slept with Angie I might never have meet Emma.

"Dinner!" My mom calls out, shocking the hell out of me. I think the last time my mother cooked dinner was when we were a real family.

"Did she say dinner?" Mila asks, peeking her head into my room.

"I think so." We both walk into the kitchen not sure what to expect.

Yup, she said dinner. On the kitchen table she has a big bowl with pasta and four placemats set up with our tan dishes. Wait why is there four spots? "Who's coming for dinner?" I ask scared of the answer.

"You'll see," My mom sings.

"It better not be who I think it is."

"Who?" Mila asks, placing a glass down for each of us.

The doorbell rings just in time for all of us to find out. Please don't let it be who I think it is. As soon as I hear her voice I know I was right. Angie walks in behind my mother wearing another tiny revealing shirt, which shows off all of her curves. I can't help but focus on her chest that looks like it is about to pop out of her shirt.

"Great," I say, finally looking away.

"What is she doing here?" Mila whispers in my ear as we head to the table.

"I'm gonna guess it's Mom's attempt at getting us back together."

"Hi Mila, Hi Nash," Angie says joining us at the table.

"Please sit, Angie. I'm so happy you came. It's been way too long since we've done this," my mom says grinning from ear to ear

"We've never done this before," I respond, still standing in front of my chair.

"What do you mean? Angie was always here for dinner when the two of you were dating." My mother motions for me to sit down. I guess she forgot it was usually take-out, and Angie and me ate in my room. "She's here now, and we are going to have a nice family dinner."

I pull the metal chair out and sit down. I don't want to be here, but I don't want to fight with them either.

"So how's work?" Angie asks Mila.

"It's a job. I'm hoping to get my GED soon and maybe sign up for some classes at the community college."

"That's awesome. How are things going with Johnny?"

"Who's Johnny?" My mother asks, twilling her spaghetti on her fork.

"He's just a friend," Mila quickly responds.

175

"He's Sam's girlfriend's brother," Angie says, twirling her own spaghetti.

"I don't like that girl. I think Sam can do better," my mom declares twitching her nose.

"What's wrong with Britney? She treats Sam good." I state.

"I'm sorry but I think Sam can do better. Mila, I hope you're not thinking about dating that boy. He's probably just like his sister."

"I'm so glad you said that. I agree with you, I don't like that girl either," Angie declares with a huge smile, a smile that is starting to get under my skin.

"You don't even know her or her brother," Mila jumps in, looking as mad as I feel.

"Why don't both of you stop your bullshit and say why you really don't like Britney," I verbalize, feeling the fire growing inside me.

"We already told you we think Sam can do bet...."

"Liar! Why don't you just say you don't like Britney because she's Emma's best friend?"

"Yeah, and?" My mother admits. "You know how I feel about that girl. I don't understand what you see in her. She's a new shiny toy you can play...."

"That's it, I'm done. I'm not gonna sit here and listen to you bash Emma again. Enjoy your family dinner without me." I get up and begin to walk towards my room. I'm not going to be part of this stupidity any longer.

"Nash, come back here right now! You are being a rude asshole."

I ignore her words and continue towards my room.

"I'll go talk to him," I overhear Angie say. Just great! "Why are you acting like this?" She asks, entering my room right behind me.

176

"Get out of my room!"

"Why are you being like this?"

"I'm really not in the mood to go through this again. Please just get out." I try my best not to raise my voice.

"It's because of that girl. Ever since you met her you've been such an ass. Pretending you're something you're not. Acting like you're above all of us."

"I'm not pretending anything. Look, I don't have time for this."

"She's nothing. She's nothing in your life. She's nothing like I was. You and I were in love once. Don't you remember? When did that end?"

"It ended when you decided to sleep with Court."

"This is all still about Court. You are still trying to get back at him." A smile comes across her face.

"This has nothing to do with Court or you."

"Then what is it about?"

"It's about love. I'm in love with Emma."

Angie's smile slowly fades away. "Why do you wanna hurt me like this?"

"I'm not trying to hurt you."

She steps forward grabbing my hands. "Why can't you forgive me?"

"I have forgiven you. I'm over everything."

"Including me?"

"Yes."

"I'm sorry, but I don't believe you. You and I have been through too much for it to be over."

"It is over. I'm in love with Emma," I say, hoping she'll get it through her head.

She lets go of my hands and steps back as tears begin to run down her face. My heart aches for her. I don't want to see her hurt like this. I take a step towards her, but she holds up her hand to stop me. "You are breaking my heart." She turns around, runs out of my house slamming the front door. I didn't want things to end like this. Why did my mom have to invite her over?

"What did you do to Angie?" My mother asks, storming into my room.

"Why did you invite her over?"

"Why shouldn't I invite her over?"

"You need to stop. I'm not getting back with her. I'm in a relationship and you need to respect that. You don't have to like it, but you need to respect it."

"You are an idiot, just like your father." She shakes her head with frustration. "You can't see when you have a great woman right in front of you." No, you need to chase after some slut…."

"Enough! I'm not Dad. And Angie is not you. I'm done having this same argument with you. Dad left you, so what? Get over it!"

My mother's eyes widen as her nose flares. She turns as red as a burning flame while she yells, "Get out of my house! GET OUT!"

I grab my keys and walk past her. I shouldn't have said what I said, but she gets me so angry. I know my mom well enough to know when she gets like this it's better to leave and give her some space.

I should have known as soon as my mom said we were having a family dinner it was going to end up bad. I jump in my pick-up and head straight towards Emma's house. I really need to see her.

I park my truck at the bottom of her street and text her, "**R u busy?**"

"**No. Y?**"

"**Can u come out?**"

"**Yeah.**"

"**I'm at the end of ur block**."

"**☺ I'll be rt there**."

Five minutes after her text she appears by my truck wearing my sweatshirt. I really love the way she looks in it.

"Hey," she says coming inside. "It's cold out there."

"Sorry. I wasn't sure if I should park in front of your house or not."

"It's cool. My parents are too busy being mad at each other to notice anything. So what's going o...." Before she can finish her question I pull her in and begin to kiss her soft lips. Having her in my arms makes everything better.

As our lips still linger on each other's I whisper, "Angie was at my house."

Emma pulls away furrowing her eyebrows, "What? Why?"

"My mom invited her over for a family dinner. I didn't know she was coming over, or I would've left earlier."

"Did anything happen?"

"Besides my mother throwing me out? No."

"What? Why?" She asks with her amber brown eyes still filled with doubt.

I explain the whole story to her. Emma listens, but seems scared to hear all the details. When she realizes nothing happened between Angie and me she finally begins to relax.

"So what are you gonna do?"

"What do you mean?"

"I mean where are you gonna stay?" She questions, with her voice full of concern.

"Oh, you mean cause my mom threw me out?"

"Yeah, why don't you seem more stressed out?"

I let out a small laugh. She really doesn't know anything about my relationship with my mom. "It's not the first time she's thrown me out. The first couple of times I went to stay at a friend's house, but now I just give her a couple of hours to cool off and then go back home. She'll act like nothing ever happened."

"Ok. Well that makes me feel better. Anyway, thanks for telling me everything."

"Of course. I told you I'm not keeping any secrets from you again." The smile warming my heart is now gone. "Are you okay? Did I say something wrong?"

"No. It's just I have to tell you something."

The last time she told me she had something to tell me, she said she was going to homecoming with Court. Please don't let it have something to do with him. "What is it?" I close my eyes and wait for her news.

* * *

Nash looks as if he knows what I have to say to him is bad news. I try to find the right words but nothing comes to mind. I can't do this. "I just was hoping you can come over for dinner on Saturday. I want my parents to really get to know you."

He opens his eyes and produces his beautiful crooked smile. "Yeah. That'll be great. Are you sure you wanna do this?"

"Yeah. I don't wanna keep our relationship a secret any longer."

"Come over here." I scoot over closer to him. He tucks me close to his chest. I look up at him and then meet his lips with mine. It's these small kisses that make me love him more each time.

We sit in his truck for another hour listening to music, talking about school, and kissing. I still can't believe a couple of weeks ago I was crying over him and now we are together and in love. Nash is all I've ever wanted. Even when I thought I was confused over Nash and Court, my heart always knew it was Nash that it really wanted. This relationship is even worth losing a friend for.

I walk back into my house smiling so hard it hurts. I don't think even my parents can ruin my happiness.

"Where have you been?" My mother asks when she spots me coming in.

"I was out with a friend."

"Which friend?"

I know I can make something up and stop this discussion from becoming a fight, but I'm tired of hiding things from her. "Nash," I say holding my breath.

"What?" My mother's eyes look as if they are about to pop out of her head. "Why were you with him?"

"We're back together."

"What? Michael, get in here!"

"What is it?" My father asks, walking into the foyer looking confused.

"Since when?" My mother asks ignoring my father's question.

"Since before homecoming," I answer.

"Are you kidding me?"

"What's been going on since before homecoming?" My father asks, still confused over what is being discussed.

"She's back with that guy Nash. The one that used her to get back at Court." My mother quickly brings my father up to speed. She turns back to face me. "Don't you remember how bad he hurt you? How can you be back with him?"

"Emma is this true?" My father asks.

"Yes. We talked about everything and he was really sorry. I decided I needed to give him another chance."

"I can't believe the words that are coming out of your mouth right now. What about Court?" My mother's anger is about to explode out of her body.

I have no idea how to answer this question. If I tell her we were never really back together she's going to know my first time was a one-night stand. At the same time I don't want her to think I cheated on Court again. "It's over between us," I finally answer.

"This can't be happening," my mother says throwing her arms in the air. "I wanted better for you than this."

"What are you talking about? Shouldn't all you want for me is to be happy?"

"Yes. That's why I don't understand why you are giving this boy, who hurt you so badly, another chance to do it again."

"Because he makes me happy. He's not going to hurt me again," I answer her hoping it's enough to change her mind.

"No. I'm sorry Emma, but I will not allow you to go out with that boy."

"What? Dad, please tell Mom she's wrong."

"I'm sorry, but this time I agree with your mother." I can't believe he's been arguing with her for the last couple of weeks about everything, but now he wants to side with her to destroy my happiness.

"You guys can't stop me from seeing him."

"You want to bet," my mother firmly states, with her arms tied together under her chest.

"I can't believe you guys are doing this. I hate you both." I run up the stairs to my room.

Why are my parents being like this? I've been walking around trying to understand why are they always arguing, really worrying about them only to have them not care one little bit about my feelings. I hate both of them.

"So I guess I'm not coming to dinner on Saturday," Nash says when I call him.

"I'm sorry. I can't believe they're acting like this."

"Do you think they can do it?"

"Do what?" I ask laying on my bed in the dark.

"Stop you from seeing me."

"No. They can't control me like that. Nash, I'm not losing you again." I grip the phone tighter to my ear as if it's him I'm getting closer to.

"Good, cause I love you and I don't wanna lose you either."

What Nash and I have is real and it's going to stay that way.

19
Panic Switch

Being with Emma has become harder than I thought it would be. Her parents won't let her go anywhere unless they know who she's going to be with and where she's going to be.

She's had Britney pick her up a couple of times, but she is not always available. Besides, she still hates me, and doesn't really like helping us out. I've tried parking my truck at the bottom and the top of her street a couple times, but the other day her father almost caught me as he drove by. It's getting exhausting, but at the same time it's all worth it to be with her.

Luckily, today she got her mom to drop her off at the café when get off my work. I can't wait to see her. These last ten minutes have been ticking by so slow. I keep looking out the window hoping to see her. I hope her mom didn't change her mind about bringing her down here. Or worse she decides to come in here with her. One look at me and she'll pull her right out of here.

Just as I think Emma might not show up she walks in looking beautiful in her brown dress with little white flowers on it and green sweater. "I love the smile that appears on your face every time you see her," Mila says coming to stand behind the counter with me.

"I can't help it, she makes me happy." I stare at her as she says hello to Britney and Sam. She looks up at me with those eyes that take my breath away.

"I can see that. I can also see you make her happy by the smile she also has on her face. Alright already, go say hello to your girl before you explode from the excitement."

I walk out from behind the counter and head straight for her. I don't give her a chance to say hello. I cradle her face in my hands and give her a long kiss hello. Having her moist warm lips on mine is all I need in this world.

I pull away and see her smile light up her face. "That was nice." She says taking hold of my hand as my heart continues to accelerate.

"Wanna go kiss some more? In my truck?" I ask, moving my eyebrows up and down.

"Yeah." I begin to lead her towards the door. I put my hand on the gold knob and just as I'm about to turn it the door flies open. I take a step back to allow Court and his friends to walk inside. He looks at Emma first and then at me and rolls his eyes in disgust. I can't help but laugh at his reaction. He really needs to get over losing Emma. Then again I couldn't get over her either. I guess I don't blame him for looking so upset.

We walk outside and the brisk air slaps me so hard it makes me gasp for air. I try to bring Emma closer to me to shield her from the cold, but she pulls away from my embrace. Why is she mad at me?

"What's wrong?" I ask.

185

"It's still all a game to you."

"What?"

"You don't think I saw how you laughed at Court's reaction to us. You still want to see him hurting. Did you know he was coming in and that's why you were trying to get me to go outside so fast?" I can't believe she still thinks I'm using her.

"Are you serious? Emma, I didn't know he was coming in at that very moment. I'm not out to get him anymore. I wish you would believe me."

"I saw you. I saw you laughing." Her body shakes with anger.

"Yeah, but it wasn't because I thought he was hurting it was because…." I begin to shake my head in disbelief. "I can't believe we're arguing about this. Emma I'm with you because I want to be with you and that's it. There's no ulterior motive."

"I wanna believe you but…." She drops her head.

I pull her back into my arms. "I know it's hard for you to trust me again, but I need you to believe me when I say what we have between us has nothing to do with Court."

"I hope it doesn't," she whispers. It kills me to know she still doesn't trust me.

* * *

My head has been mixed up all day. I've been having trouble concentrating in all of my classes. I didn't mean to get so mad at Nash last night, but I can't help feeling scared of being used again. I want to believe him when he tells me he loves me, but there's this part of me that keeps thinking it's all a trick. Am I ever really going be able to fully trust him?

I walk into my last class feeling mentally exhausted. I'm really not in the mood to deal with anything else today, including Court. He pretty much has been ignoring me since our big fight. I wish I could say I didn't care, but I do. I really miss his friendship. He was an important person in my life.

He walks in with Christy attached to his hip, like she's been since the end of our friendship. She always makes sure to flash me an evil smile before she takes her seat.

This time instead of sitting right away she leans into Court and says loud enough for me to hear all the way in the back of the room, "Oh Court, did I leave my white sweater in your room last night?" My insides curl with anger.

"I think it is, I'll check." He smiles and then quickly glances my way. I instantly look out the window and pretend not to notice him. I will not allow him to see that any of this affects me.

The next forty-five minutes are hell. I have to watch Christy and him whisper in each other's ear. I'm not sure I'm going to be able to survive another seven months in this class. I wonder if it's too late to transfer. When the bell finally rings I grab my bag and try my best to be the first one to escape the room. I'm happy this day is finally over.

"You look happy," Britney says, meeting me at my locker.

"I'm so sick of English class. I guess Court and Christy are now hooking up again."

"No way. There's no way. I saw them at the café last night and he wasn't acting like he was into her at all. In fact he was talking to another girl," she states looking for something in her bag.

"Really? Then why did she ask him if she left her sweater in his room last night."

"I don't know. But I'm telling you he was hanging out with some other girl. I think you know her. She's that girl he hung out with at Fairland Park after you guys broke up."

"Rebecca?" I ask surprised.

"I think that's her name." I can't believe Court is working with Christy to get to me. What a jerk. Maybe it is a good thing he's out of my life. "Anyway they both looked pretty cozy together."

"And you say Christy was there?"

"Yeah, she was in the corner staring at them with pure hatred in her eyes. It was kind of sad to see. Court is never going to give that girl the attention she so badly wants," Britney says walking alongside me.

"I don't feel bad for her. Christy deserves a lot more than that."

We both walk out of the building. It's October but feels more like January. All of a sudden, my body begins to warm up when I spot Nash sitting in his truck right outside the doors. He's exactly who I need to see.

"What is he doing here?" Britney asks, with annoyance in her voice.

"When are you going to stop hating him?"

"I really don't know."

Why can't one person in my life support my relationship with Nash? They all make me feel as if it's us against the world. "I'm sorry you feel that way. I'll call you later."

I jump into his truck hoping he'll help me shake this day off. "Hey, this is a nice surprise," I say closing my door.

"I'm glad." He leans in and gives me a sweet kiss making every butterfly in my stomach wake up and whirl around. "So what time do you have to be home?"

"It doesn't matter. I'll just tell them I had work to do in the library."

"Cool. I don't have to be at work till six. How about we go get something to eat?"

"Sounds perfect."

He starts to drive down the parking lot. "Emma, I really stopped by to make sure we were good. You know, after yesterday. I hate thinking that you doubt me," his eyes look lost.

"I don't doubt you. But I can't help feeling scared sometimes."

"No, I understand. I would feel the same way if it was the other way around." He smiles making me feel safe again. "So, is Barney's Burger Palace cool with you?"

"Yeah."

"Me too. My mother used to work at the Inn across the street from there. Mila, Ben and me used to wait for her at Barney's all the time. We always ordered the same thing, three double cheese burgers with onion rings." I love hearing stories about when he was kid. It makes me feel closer to him.

"So your mom used to work at the Harbor's Inn?"

"Yeah, you know the place?"

"Yeah, sometimes I go to their restaurant with my parents, but I always wish we would go to Barney's instead."

"Really. And I always wanted to go to the restaurant in the Inn, but it's too expensive at least that's what my mom always said."

"It is a bit overpriced for stuffy food."

"You know what that inn is famous for? Right?" He asks moving his eyebrows up and down as he gives me a sly grin.

I shake my head.

"It's famous for married people who are having an affair to meet up with their lovers."

"No way!"

"Yes it is. Mila, Ben and me used to always sit at the window in Barney's trying to figure out who was cheating on their spouses."

I start laughing picturing them looking out the window as if they were watching a reality television show.

We jump out of his truck and hold hands as we walk towards the entrance. This is turning out to be a great day. "How about you go get us a table and I'll order our food," he says opening the door for me.

"Okay."

"What do you want?"

I smile and say, "A double cheese burger and onion rings."

"God, I love you." He grabs my face with his cold hands and gives me a kiss.

I walk on the blue and white tiled floor looking for the perfect table. I find it right by the window that faces the Inn's parking lot. Maybe we'll get to see some couples sneaking out of the Inn. I sit in the blue vinyl seat and imagine Nash, Mila and Ben sitting here waiting for their mother. It all makes my whole body smile.

I look out at the beautiful brisk day when all of a sudden I feel a brick hits me in the face. I can't believe what my eyes are seeing. There is no way I'm seeing this.

My mother's car is sitting in the Inn's parking lot right next to Peter Dobberson's BMW. I would have never noticed if I didn't see my mother passionately hugging Mr. Dobberson right before she gets into her car.

I can't believe this—my mother is having an affair with Court's father. This can't be happening. Please don't let this be happening.

"Are you okay?" Nash asks brining our tray to the table.

"No. I have to get out of here."

"Why. What happened?"

"I just have to go," I say getting up. "I can't breathe. There's no air in here. I need to get out of here. Please lets just go."

"Okay. But first tell me what's wrong."

"Look," I say pointing towards the Inn's parking lot. But their cars are already gone.

"What is it?"

I can't hold back my tears any longer. "My mother, Court's father"

"What about your mother and Court's father."

"They were both at the Inn. I think they're having an affair. I can't breathe. I have to go outside." I walk past him and rush out the door almost knocking into a little kid and his father.

I step out on the sidewalk and try to breathe, but the damn air will not go in. I can't take this. Why is this happening? Oh my God, does my father know? Maybe this is why they've been fighting so much.

"Emma! Emma, wait stop!" Nash calls out.

I don't even realize I'm walking down the street so fast. I just have to get away from here. "AAAAAAHHHH!" I let out.

"Emma." Nash finally stops me, turns me around, and lets me fall into his arms.

"Why is she doing this? Why with him? Isn't my dad good enough for her?"

"Maybe they weren't there for what you're thinking. The Inn has a restaurant. Remember? Maybe they were there getting some lunch."

"No. They were there to hook up. I saw them. I saw the way he hugged her. You even said that the Inn is famous for that. I can't believe this is happening. I hate her! How can she do this to our family?"

"There has to be an explanation. Why don't you go talk to her."

"I don't wanna talk to her. I never wanna talk to her again." I continue to cry in his arms as he holds me up. Why is this happening?

Nash and I drive around as my brain tries to deal with what I saw. My heart aches for my father and burns for my mother. The hatred that is building inside me is beginning to really hurt.

"I don't wanna leave you like this. I'll call out from work."

"No. I'll be okay. I just have to deal with this. I think it's time I go home."

"Are you sure?" He asks, taking my hand in his.

"Yeah." But I'm not sure I am. I have no idea what I'm going to say when I see my mother. I don't even know how I'm ever going to be able to look into her evil lying eyes again.

"Where do you want me to drop you off?"

"In front of my house. I don't care anymore."

"Okay."

Nash pulls up right in front of my house as my stomach tries to push out the non-existing contents in it. How am I going to do this? "Are you sure you don't want me to stay with you?"

"No, I'll be okay." I turn around to look at Nash, who tries to give me a small grin. I so badly just want to bury my head into his chest and cry my eyes out again. "I'm sorry I ruined our meal."

"You didn't ruin anything. Look, I get off at nine thirty. If you need anything just call me. I'll be here as fast as I can. Or if you need me earlier I'll just leave. I don't care."

"Thank you. I love you."

"I love you too." He leans forward and gives me a kiss. I close my eyes and try to hold on to that kiss for as long as I can.

I jump out of Nash's truck and begin to walk towards my house feeling as if I'm about to face my execution. I wonder if my father knows yet. What if he doesn't know? Should I be the one to tell him? Oh God, I have no idea what to do.

I open the door and am surprised to hear the television is on. "Emma is that you?" My mother calls out. *Who else would it be?*

"Yeah."

I walk into the living room thinking I would find her watching TV by herself, but she's not. My father is sitting right next to her with his arm around her shoulders. I have to fight back my tears that are trying to rip out their way out of my eyes.

I can't believe she can sit there with him acting like she hasn't done anything wrong. She's disgusting. She's the most disgusting human being I know.

"Where were you? We were starting to get worried," she asks getting up from the couch.

I stand up straight and try my best not to show any rage in my voice as I say, "I was with Nash."

193

My father snaps his head my way as my mother says, "I hope you didn't say what I think you said."

"I did say it. So deal with it."

"Young lady, I know you're not talking to your mother like that." My father snaps. Why doesn't he know what's going on under his own nose? *Come on Dad open your eyes and see what Mom is doing to you.*

"I'm going to my room."

"We're not finish talking about this," My mother .

"I don't really care. I'm done talking about this!"

"That's it you're grounded!"

"Whatever!" I begin to run up the stairs before I tell my mother what I saw this afternoon.

"Can you believe her?" I hear my mother ask my father. I would like to ask my father the same question about my adulteress mother.

As soon as my body hits my bed my eyes begin to release my burning tears. This is all too much. It feels like a nightmare I can't wake up from. Where do I go from here?

20
Roll On

I wish there was something I could do to make everything better for Emma. I hate to see her in this much pain. It was different for me when my father cheated on my mother. I always knew my father was an asshole, so it wasn't a huge surprise when he left all of us for another woman.

It's unreal to think Emma's mom and Court's dad are having an affair. Why did her mom have to pick him? What if they end up together? Court will be in our lives again. I can't believe that's even crossing my mind right now. I should only be thinking about being there for Emma. She really needs me right now.

Oh man, poor Mr. Paige when he finds out. I know how I felt when I found out about Angie. My heart was shattered in a million pieces, and my trust was beaten to shreds; that must of been how my mom felt too. I never really thought about the way she felt when she found out about my father. I remember her crying all the time, but I was too busy worrying about myself to be there for her. I do suck.

It must be how she still feels, but it must be ten times worse for her since she is still in love with my asshole father. No wonder she's been so hard on me about breaking up with Angie.

I quickly call Emma when I get off my shift. She manages to say she's okay and is going to bed. I know she's not, but all I could do right now is give her space. It's more than any of us gave my mom.

"Thank you for letting me do this," I hear my mom say, as I walk through my front door.

Who the hell is here with her? Please don't let it be Angie again. I can't deal with seeing her right now. I walk into the kitchen and see my mom putting hair dye in my sister's hair.

"Hey hon," my mom says looking happy.

"What are you guys doing?"

"Mom is coloring my hair dark cherry red."

"Why?"

"Because we were bored," Mila answers, as if it's a normal response. "How was work?"

"Ok, I guess. Well I'm beat. I'll see you guys later." I look over at my mom, who's eyes are full of joy, but at the same time sadness. I feel like I understand her a bit more now. I walk over and give her a quick kiss on the top of her head.

"What was that for?" She asks looking at me confused.

"I love you. That's all." Her eyes become glassy, which warms and breaks my heart at the same time. I really have to start being a better son. I look over at Mila, who also looks as if she's about to cry. "Okay goodnight," I say, and walk towards my room before I join them in a tear fest.

It might be time to tell my mother about what Angie did to me. I really didn't want to throw Angie under the bus like that, but I have no choice if I want all the women in my life to get along.

* * *

I walk out of my house this morning before either one of my parents is up. I don't know how to face them knowing what I know. Most of all I don't know if I could control my anger around my mother. I still can't believe she is having an affair.

This is all my fault. If I had never agreed to be Court's girlfriend last spring our parents would have never reunited, and I wouldn't be here about to lose my entire family.

"Thanks for picking me up this early," I say, getting into Britney's car.

"No problem. Is everything ok? Did something happen with Nash?"

"Why do you always assume it has to do with Nash?"

"I don't know." She turns to look at the road, biting her lower lip. "I'm sorry, is everything okay?"

"Not really." I don't want to think about it anymore. But I can't help it. Every time I close my eyes I see my mother in Mr. Dobberson's arms.

"Do you wanna talk about it?"

"Not really." The truth is I'm embarrassed to tell her. My parents are supposed to be the perfect couple. I mean they're a little boring, but that's what makes them perfect. They're supposed to be the couple who stays together forever.

"Okay, but if you do wanna talk I'm here for you," Britney says looking hurt.

"Thanks. I will tell you as soon as I clear it up in my head first."

I hate my parents for putting me in this situation. Actually, I only hate my mother, and I feel so bad for my father. I still remember his eyes when I saw him crying. Now I know why he looked so hurt.

I walk into school with my heart aching with anger and sadness. I don't think I can do this today. Why didn't I try to convince Britney to skip school with me? Maybe it's not too late. "Hey Brit?"

"Yeah?"

"How about we…."

"Emma, can I talk to you?" I hear a familiar voice say behind me. I turn around slowly and see Court standing there with his eyes filled with agony. Ohmigod, does he also know about our parents?

"A…a…yeah, sure."

"I'll see you guys later," Britney sings, giving me one of her big goofy smiles. I wish she would stop hoping that Court and me would get back together.

"What's up?" I ask, when Britney is far enough away not to hear us.

"I guess there's only one way to say this." *Oh no, he does know*. I close my eyes and try to breathe. "I'm sorry for being such an ass lately."

"What?" I open my eyes wide.

"I was a jerk. You and I were good friends and I'm sorry I reacted the way I did. I guess I was hurt when you picked him over me again." I can't believe he's actually apologizing to me.

"Is that why you've been using Christy to get me jealous?"

He looks down at his new expensive sneakers. "Yeah." He shoots his baby blue eyes back up towards me and says, "I hate to admit I was trying to hurt you. I wanted you to feel the same pain I felt. But look, those games are over. I wanna be your friend again. And I want you to know if you ever need a shoulder to lean on I'm here for you."

His words warm my heart and make the anger that is drilling a hole in it fill up with joy. At the same time I don't understand where all this is coming from. Does he know what's going on or not? I don't get it.

"So what do you say? Do you think we can be friends again?" He asks with his perfect smile.

I look up at him and know it's all I've ever wanted. "Yeah."

"Come here." He pulls me into his arms and gives me a tight hug. It feels so good to be in his warm embrace again. I can't help but wonder if he's still going to want to be my friend when he finds out our parents are doing it.

Ohmigod, what if our parents get married? We'll be brother and sister. I love Court, but I don't want him to be my brother. I like being the only child, ok maybe I haven't always, but I like it now.

"Are you okay?" Court asks as I pull away.

"Yeah, just overwhelmed over all of this."

"I know what you mean. Well I better get to class. I'll see you in English class."

"Okay." I watch Court walk away and catch up to his other friends. It's just a little weird he chooses the day after I caught our parents together to want to be friends again. I wish I knew what he knew.

21
<u>City On Down</u>

Emma's pain has actually made our relationship better. She doesn't care that her parents don't want us to be together anymore. She breaks their rules almost every day, gets punished, but still comes out to see me.

I'm not saying I'm happy about what she's going through, but I like how close we've gotten over it. Today I have a huge surprise for her. Hopefully, she'll want to break a couple more rules. I've been looking for something perfect to help her, and I hope this surprise will do it.

I pull up in front of her house just as she's slamming her front door. Emma runs down towards my truck with her dark brown hair flying behind her. "Drive," she says jumping in.

Her mother walks out the door and yells, "Emma, get back here right now!"

"Just drive!"

"Is everything okay?"

"No. She tried to tell me how my behavior is disturbing her. She should talk. Her behavior is disturbing me," Emma says, as her body shakes with anger.

"Have you tried to talk to her?"

"I do not wanna talk to that woman. Just having to look her in the eyes pisses me off. I don't wanna talk about her anymore. Please tell me we're going somewhere I can get my mind off of everything."

"Actually, I had an idea, but if we go where I'm planning to take you I won't be able to bring you back by your curfew."

She huffs out a small laugh, "You think I care? I'm supposed to be grounded right now. I wanna go anywhere with you."

"I was hoping you'd say that. Alright then, lets get out of this town," I announce getting onto the highway.

"Where are we going?"

"New York City."

A huge smile comes across her face as her eyes light up. "Really? Why?"

"You'll see."

We take the two-hour trip into the city talking about school, our summer before our break up, and of course Ben and Jason. The whole time I hold her hand hoping she can feel how much I love her.

Since we have time I decide to drive through Time Square. All the lights shine making it seem like it's still daytime outside. With excitement in her eyes Emma looks out the window pointing at everything.

"This is beautiful. I would love to live here one day," Emma says, jumping in her seat.

"Me too, but not in this area. I'm more of a downtown kind of guy."

"Is that where we are going?"

"Yeah."

"This is so exciting."

We drive for another thirty minutes until I finally find the street I'm looking for in Greenwich Village. I make sure to read all the parking rules. I have to make sure it's okay to park and not get towed. I've watched way too many episodes of Parking Wars to just park anywhere.

"You ready?" I ask Emma, who looks up and down the street that is a lot darker than what we just drove through.

"Yeah."

We jump out of my truck, I grab her hand, and begin to lead her across the street toward the Bowery Ballroom, a small Manhattan venue that plays live music. We reach the long line of people just as they begin to enter.

"Who are we seeing?" Emma asks leaning into me shivering so hard her teeth are clattering.

"O.A.R."

"What?! Are you serious?" She jumps out of my arms full of excitement.

"Yeah," I laugh.

She jumps back into my arms wrapping her arms around my neck and kisses me with her amazing soft lips, making every part of me tingle with love. "I love you!"

"I love you too."

I'm so happy to see her smile again. All I want is for her to smile like this all the time.

* * *

I always thought venues in Manhattan would be a lot bigger but The Bowery Ballroom is just as small as Cake. Unlike Cake, it has a second floor that has balcony seats. I still can't believe I'm in here. It's going to be amazing to see O.A.R this close up. Nash really is the best boyfriend for doing this. It is helping me take my mind off the whole situation with my mother. It's exactly what I needed.

Nash grabs my hand tight and wiggles us through the people to stand right in front of the stage. My heart pumps so loud I swear I can hear it in my ears.

He stands behind me and locks his arms around my waist. It reminds me of the first time we ever saw a concert together. I knew then I was going to fall deeply in love with him.

"You ready for an experience you'll never forget?" He whispers in my ear, producing goose bumps all over my body.

I nod just as the lights lower and O.A.R takes the stage. I can't stop my body from jumping up and down. I can't believe they are right in front of me. We all begin to sing *Love and Memory* with them. The lead singer Marc looks right into my eyes as he sings the chorus, sending my head and heart into a wild whirlwind.

I turn my head to look at Nash and like a little girl I begin to scream, "Ohmigod, did you see that? Marc looked at me! He looked at me!" Nash nods giving me the crooked smile I love so much. I turn my whole body around and begin to kiss him.

O.A.R sings song after song making the crowd and me go wild. Every so often I turn around to kiss Nash. This is turning out to be the best night of my life. I never thought I could have this much fun with all that's going on in my heart.

At the end of the show I can't help but feel sad. I wish it would've gone on all night long.

"So I take it you had fun," Nash says taking my hand in his as we exit.

"Yes! This had to be the best show ever. Thank you so much."

"My pleasure. I'm glad you had a good time."

As soon as I enter Nash's truck I check my phone and see I have eighteen phone calls from my parents with eighteen voice messages. I listen to the first one that pretty much is demanding me to come home. I decide to ignore the rest of them, which I'm sure say the same thing.

"Is everything okay?" Nash asks, giving me a quick glance as we get on the Henry Hudson Parkway.

"Yeah."

"Are you gonna be in trouble when you get home?"

"Probably, but I don't care. To be honest, I wish I didn't have to go home at all."

"It's going to be okay. I promise."

I want to believe him, but I can't. There is no way this is going to be okay; the family I know will sooner or later no longer exist.

I lean back on my seat watching all the lights swim by. My eyelids become heavier with each minute that passes. I close my eyes for a second and open them again to see Nash staring at me. "I didn't wanna wake you up." I turn my head and feel my stomach drop. We are sitting right in front of my house.

"I don't wanna go in," I whisper.

"I know. I wish I could take you home with me, but I'm afraid my mom would have an issue with that."

"Is there any other place else you can take me? Please. I really can't go in there yet," I beg.

He starts his truck and drives away before my parents even have a chance to look out the window. "Let me call Leo, maybe he'll let us stay there."

I listen with my fingers crossed. I really do not want to go home and face my parents. I'm afraid I'll say something I shouldn't. It's been so hard not to say anything for this long.

"He said we can stay at his place tonight, but tomorrow I'm gonna have to drive you home."

"That's fine. I'll deal with them tomorrow." I put my head on his shoulder and feel safe again.

22
Cling and Clatter

Emma and me enter Leo's house at 3:30 in the morning. Jen and Leo greet us in their pajamas. They both look so tired. I feel bad for waking them up. They offer us something to eat, but we both refuse. I'm exhausted from the drive.

We walk straight into the same room where I first told her I loved her. We both stare at the bed for a minute not saying anything. The last time we laid on it we almost had sex.

"I can sleep on the floor if you want me too," I finally say breaking the silence.

"Of course not. All I want to do is fall asleep in your arms." She looks at me with her amber brown eyes lost in pain.

I take off my sweatshirt and T-shirt, while she takes off her sweatshirt and jeans. She stands there in only her fitted white tee and cute blue panties. My body becomes erect by just looking at her. I have to talk myself into thinking about something horrible to calm myself down. Tonight is not the right night to try anything with her.

We both go under the covers at the same time. "Do you wanna watch some TV?" I ask, feeling her legs touch mine, which are now bare after removing my jeans too.

She shakes her head. Emma turns to her side to look out the window. I wrap my arms around her warm body and tuck her real close to me. She smells so good. I wish there was a way for me to take away all her pain.

She turns around to face me, and with the help of the moonlight I see her beautiful face. "I love you," she whispers.

"I love you too." She brings her lips to mine and begins to kiss me.

Our kissing starts off slow, but slowly becomes deeper as her tongue enters my mouth to dance with mine. Before I know it her hands begin to travel up and down my back making my body want more.

I slowly sneak my hand under her shirt. Every part of me once again gets way too excited. I trail my finger on her stomach for a while, afraid if I continue to go up she'll stop me.

Her body presses against me as she moans in my ear making every hair on my arms rise with excitement. My hand continues to go up her shirt until I am cupping her breast. Emma moans louder. I want her so bad it hurts.

I climb on top of her and her legs instantly wrap around my body. We both begin to grind to the same rhythm. The thought of being inside her drives me crazy.

"I want you," Emma says between kisses. "I want to feel you inside me. I want to feel anything but the pain I've been feeling." All at once my body turns cold. I get off her. "What's wrong?"

"We can't do this right now."

She sits up with rage filling her body. "I can't believe you are doing this to me again. Every single time we have come close to taking it one step further you reject me. Why? Am I still part of a game for you?"

"What? No. Emma there's nothing more I wanna do than be with you, but I don't want to do it like this. Not while you're dealing with what's going on with your parents." I pull her close to me. "I love you and when you and I take it to the next level I want it to be because we wanna be together and for no other reason."

"But I do want to be with you."

"No. You just want to be with me to mask the pain you're feeling."

"That's not why I wanted…." Tears quickly stream down her face. She begins to sob harder as I pull her in closer. Her head falls onto my chest. I hold her in my arms allowing her to cry. We both stay in each other's arms until we fall asleep.

I try opening my eyelids that feel like they have been glued down. My eyes finally open to see Emma lying next to me. Somehow she looks even prettier in the morning.

"You're cute when you're sleeping," She says, tracing the tattoo on my back making all of my skin tingle. "I want one."

"A tattoo?"

"Yeah. I wanna be your first customer."

"You got it." Her phone vibrates on the nightstand on her side of the bed. I didn't even realize she had put it there. "Are you gonna get that?" I motion towards it with my chin.

"No. It's probably my parents for the six hundredth time."

"Maybe you should let them know you're okay."

"But I'm not." She digs her face in her pillow while I rub her back this time. She pops her head back up and says, "But you're also right."

She turns around and picks up her phone. Her eyes open wide while she checks who called her. A smile appears on her face as she sits up. "It wasn't my parents, it was Court."

Court? Why the hell is he calling her? Emma dials his number and waits for him to answer as she swings her legs off the side of the bed.

"Hey. You called me?"

She listens holding the phone very close to her ear.

"I'm sorry they called you. They shouldn't have done that."

She listens some more nodding her head.

"I'm okay. I'm just dealing with some stuff."

Emma listens again while I fight every bone in my body not to grab the phone from her.

"Thank you. Yeah, I'll be heading home soon. Thanks for checking on me. I'll talk to you later. Bye."

I'm trying hard to fight the fury that seems to be burning through each of my muscles.

She turns around with a small smile and says, "Can you believe my parents called him looking for me?"

"Didn't he tell them you guys are no longer friends?"

"Actually we are friends again."

"When did this happen?" I try my best to not sound irritated, but my voice gives me away.

"The day after I found out what my mother and his dad have been up to. He apologized for everything. I keep wondering if he knows what I know, and is just scared to tell me."

"Maybe. You should ask him."

"Are you mad?" She asks, looking perplexed.

"No. I mean, it bugs me out that he called you." I also want to tell her I didn't like her reaction, or how quick she called him back.

"Well don't worry about it. He knows I'm with you. He respects that."

"I hope so." She crawls back next to me and gives me a sweet morning kiss. I really hope she's right.

"I hate to ruin our fun, but I better get you home. You're parents already hate me enough, I'm sure after last night they're gonna want me dead.

"I guess you're right." She gets up slowly and begins to get dressed. I really don't want to take her home, but I don't want her to be in more trouble than she already is in. Besides I don't want her parents to call Court again.

We both thank Leo and Jen for letting us spend the night. I can tell they are both still shocked Emma stayed over. They both know how much her parents disapprove of me.

The ride to her house is a quiet one. I know Emma is thinking about what waits for her at home, while all I can think about is what almost happened last night. As if Emma can read my mind she says, "I understand why you stopped us from going any further last night. And I thank you."

"It wouldn't have been right." I pull up in front of her house and already begin to miss her.

She looks at me and places her hand on top of mine. "I want you to know I am ready to take that next step with you. Last night might have not been right, but I'm ready for it to be right. There's just a couple things I need to talk to you about fir…." I lean forward and begin to kiss her. The taste of her sweet lips drives me wild again. I take my hand and place it behind her head to bring her in for a deeper kiss.

Our lips tango with each other, and all I want to do is start my truck and take her with me. But I don't get a chance to. The door opens and a strong arm pulls Emma away from me. I look up and see Mr. Paige's furious eyes shooting daggers at me.

"Dad! What are you doing?"

"You want to act like a little girl, I will treat you like a little girl." He pulls her out of my truck making her bag spill out all of its contents. We all look at my front seat that contains Emma's life. She frees herself from her dad's grip and quickly starts putting everything back into her bag. But it's too late, we all see the birth control container.

Emma's dad looks at me with even more rage in his dark eyes. He makes a fist with his hand as his nostrils open wide with each breath he takes. I'm sure he wants to pull me out of the truck too. "Nash, I'll call you later," Emma says.

"No she won't! You better stay away from my daughter!" He slams my door before I have a chance to respond. I drive away not really letting his words affect me as much as seeing Emma's birth control does. I guess she is ready for us to take it to the next step.

* * *

I can't believe my father just did that, or that he saw my birth control. I really hope he didn't but I'm sure he did. I walk ahead of him trying to rush inside before he starts yelling at me in the middle of the driveway.

"Emma!" My mother says rushing to my side. Her eyes are swollen. She must have been crying all night long. I want to feel bad for her, but I don't. All of this is her fault. "Where have you been?"

"Out!"

"Is that all you can say? We have been here worried sick to death about you."

"Whatever." If this would have happened a couple weeks ago I would have been shaking in my boots, but now I really don't care. There is nothing she can say that will hurt me.

"ENOUGH!" My father yells. His anger however, does send waves of fear throughout my body. "I will not allow you to talk to your mother that way. I am done with your attitude. And after what I saw out there proves you're not the daughter I know."

"What did you see out there?" My mother asks with agony in her voice.

"It's nothing," he responds.

"Go ahead and tell her. She already knows," I say, turning those waves of fear into waves of anger.

"What do I already know?" My mother asks staring at my father and me.

"That I'm on birth control."

"I do know."

"How did you know?" My father asks.

"Who do you think bought them for me. After she found out I slept with Court she took me to her doctor to be put on them." I'm tired of keeping secrets in this house.

"Court? Wait, why didn't you tell me?" My father's voice begins to fill with anger again.

"I got you those pills because I thought you were sleeping with Court and not that boy."

"His name is Nash. And we are not sleeping together."

"I still don't understand why I wasn't told!" My father says slamming his fist against the wall.

Tears begin to escape my eyes because I know what I'm going to say next is really going to tear his heart apart. "Because Mom likes to keep secrets. Things she thinks no one knows about. But Mom I do know!"

My mother's face loses all it's color as she falls down onto a chair. "You do know, don't you?"

"Yeah, I know."

"How did you find out?" My father asks shocking me.

"You know too?" I ask, falling back against the wall. I didn't expect him to know. How did he find out? Why isn't he mad? "Aren't you angry?"

"A little. I'm more scared than anything," he admits.

"How did you find out?" My mother asks still looking pale.

"I saw you."

"Huh?"

"Does Mrs. Dobberson know?"

"She does. But what does she have to do with this?" I don't even know how my father can ask me that. Maybe he doesn't know everything I do.

"Wait a minute. What do you mean you saw me?" My mother questions me.

"I saw you and Mr. Dobberson holding each other right outside of Harbor's Inn. How could you do this to our family?" I can no longer stop myself from crying. My mother rushes to my side and tries to hold me. I pull away. "I saw you Mom, and maybe Dad can forgive you but I can't."

"Emma, I'm sorry but I don't understand what you think you saw."

"I SAW YOU AND COURT'S DAD! I know you're having an affair!"

"What!?" Both of my parents say at the same time.

"You and Mr. Dobberson are sleeping together. I'm sorry Dad if you didn't...."

"Your mother is not having an affair," My father states.

"But I saw her with Mr. Dobberson. I was across the street at Barney's Burger Palace and I saw them together, hugging right before they entered their separate cars."

"What you didn't see is Catherine and me were already in the cars," My father says shaking his head.

"Huh?" Is he lying to me so I won't be angry anymore? "I don't get it. You were there?"

"Yes. We all went to lunch together. I asked them to join your mother and I so maybe they could help me convince your mother to...."

"Michael, please let me be the one to tell her." My mother steps close to me again with tears building in her eyes. Why do I feel what she's about to tell me is going to be worse than what I believed to be true? "When we got back from the Hamptons I got a phone call from the doctor to let me know they found a lump in my breast."

"What?" My legs can no longer hold me up.

"They found a lump in my left breast. I wanted to ignore it hoping it would just go away, but it didn't. Your father asked the Dobbersons to help talk to me, since Cathy had gone through her own breast cancer scare. They convinced me I had to find out what was going on with my body. So I had a biopsy done, while you were at school."

"And?" I ask, scared to death to hear the next words to come out of her mouth.

"I have breast cancer sweetie," she says, walking towards me with tears streaming down her face.

I move right before she can reach me. She can't be telling me the truth. "No. No. No, no, no. This can't be true. It can't!" There is no air in this house. I feel like I'm going under a big wave of reality. I'm suffocating. "I need to get out of here!" I grab my mother's keys off the hook and run towards her car. I need to get away from this house.

"Emma!" My father yells after me.

I open the door as fast as I can and drive off before he can stop me. This can't be happening again. I can't deal with this again. I put the radio up and try to let Led Zeppelin erase all the thoughts I'm having.

I drive until I reach the cemetery. My head feels like it's going to explode with all the thoughts running through my mind. I run straight towards Jason's headstone with a lump burning it's way through my throat.

"Jason I need your help. Please. I need you to tell who ever is up there, if it's God or someone else, I need you to ask him or her not to take my mother. Please! I can't lose her. Please, I can't go through this again. I can't lose another person in my life. Please Jason. Please ask them to help my mother get well. Please Jason. Tell them I'll do anything. I can't lose my mother. AAAAAAHHHH!" I scream as the truth rips through my body. My mother…I can't lose my mother. I fall onto my knees crying harder than I ever have.

23
Rip Tide

All I did at work was think about Emma. I hope she's okay. I tried calling her, but she didn't answer. Maybe her parents took her phone away. I'm scared they are going to do everything they can to keep us apart.

"Want a beer?" Mila asks when I arrive home with Sam.

"Yeah thanks. Where's mom?" Mila tosses me a can. I open it and drink it all up in two gulps. I motion for another one and Mila throws me a can.

"She had to work. So, how was the show last night?" Mila asks opening her can.

"Amazing. Thanks for getting me the tickets."

"No problem. Did Emma have a good time?"

"Yup," I say sitting on the couch next to her.

"Good. Now are you gonna tell me why you didn't come home last night?" Mila raises one eyebrow higher than the other. When she does that she reminds me of Ben.

"I stayed at Leo's house," I admit, taking another huge gulp of beer.

"By yourself?"

I immediately smile. "No."

"You didn't tell me you spent the night with Emma," Sam says, getting as excited as Mila.

"I did. But not in the way you guys are thinking."

"How did Emma's parents react when she got home this morning?" Mila asks, tucking her legs up to her chest.

"Let's just say her dad was a little more than mad. He warned me not to ever see her again."

"Do you blame him?"

"I think he was more upset about what fell out of her bag." Why did I just say that? I blame the beer.

"What came out of her bag?" Mila's eyes open wider. I just smile and before I know it she guesses, "She's on the pill and the container fell out of her bag."

"How do you know?" I ask, shocked.

"How do you think Dad found out I was having sex?"

"I don't wanna know this," I state, putting up my hand to stop her from talking.

"Oh man, her dad found out about her birth control. I bet he's really gonna be mad at her mom now." Sam says confusing me.

"Why would he be mad at her mom?" Mila asks.

"She's the one that got it for her after she found out Emma had...." Sam stops speaking when he see's the confusion on my face. "Forget it. I don't know what I'm saying."

"No. When she found Emma had what?" I stand up with my heart beating harder. I'm not sure I want to know.

"Nothing," Sam answers looking away. Now I know he's hiding something.

"Sam, tell me what the fuck Emma had!"

"I'm sorry. I thought you knew." He closes his eyes and reopens one as he reveals, "Emma's mom put her on the pill after she found out she slept with Court."

217

"You're lying." He has to be lying. There is no way Emma would sleep with Court. She wouldn't do that.

"I…I…look, Nash I really thought you knew. Britney even thought you knew, that's why she told me."

"When the hell did this happen?"

"Nash I…."

"TELL ME!" I can't help yelling as my world crumbles right in front of my eyes.

"When they were in Hamptons."

How could Emma not tell me? This is bullshit. I grab my keys and begin to head towards door.

"Where are you going?" Mila asks, running to stand in front of me.

"To talk to Emma. I need to get to the bottom of this."

"You can't. She's in trouble right now, and I'm sure they won't let you talk to her."

"Then I'm going to beat Court's head in."

"You can't do that either."

"Fine. I just have to get out of here," I hiss, feeling dizzy with rage.

"You can't."

"Mila get out of my way!"

"No. You've been drinking and I'm not letting you go," she says putting her arms up to block the front door.

"Mila!"

"I said no! I already lost one brother because I couldn't stop him from doing something stupid. I'm not gonna lose another one."

"I have to go talk to her," my voice begins to crack.

"Fine, but not today. Tomorrow, after school. Please," she begs.

I slam my keys on the table by the door and storm to my room. My heart is breaking into a million pieces again. First Angie and now Emma, why do they all lie to me. I really loved her. Why would she do this to me? She's not the girl I thought she was.

* * *

I'm afraid to look at mother after all the pain I've been causing her. It kills me to know all the hatred I was feeling towards her. I slowly open the door, afraid I'll be attacked as soon as I put one foot inside, although I do deserve to be yelled at.

To my surprise my house seems to be empty. Where did they go? Ohmigod, what if something happened to my mother? I quickly glance at my phone but only see three missed calls from Nash. I can't talk to him yet.

"She's upstairs," My father says, coming in from the kitchen. Suddenly, I realize the struggle he's been dealing with all this time. Now I understand why he's been so mad at my mother. He doesn't want to lose her either. I quickly give him a tight hug. I wish I could feel safe in his arms the same way I did when I was a little girl, but I can't. "Go up and talk to her."

I walk up the stairs with a cloud of shame hanging over me. I take a deep breath in right before I open my parent's bedroom door.

My mother sits up on her bed when she sees me. She no longer looks like this monster I had made her out to be. She looks weak and broken. "Are you okay?" She asks me.

A flood of sorrow enters my body and before I can answer I begin to cry. "I-don't-want-you-die," I utter between sobs. I crawl on the bed next to her.

"Oh honey, I'm not going to die. Well at least not any time soon." I put my head on her chest, as my tears blind my vision. "I'm going to fight this cancer thing with everything I've got. I'm not going anywhere, I promise you."

"Please don't. I love you Mommy."

"I love you too." She places a kiss on my head and makes me feel safe again.

She explains everything to me. How they are going to give her a double mastectomy. Depending on her surgery it will determine if she needs chemo or not, which she already warns me will be the worst part. She jokes about how she's looking forward to getting a blond wig since she's always wanted to be a blond.

"No. I think you should go red," I say, still lying in her arms.

"How about I get one in each color? One day I can be blond the next a red head."

"Sounds perfect."

"You know what's the best part of all this?"

No matter how much I try to think of something, I can't think of anything being the best part of all of this. "What?"

"I'll finally get you to wear pink, even if it is just a ribbon." We both start laughing, which feels good but at the same time wrong. I promise I will wear pink everyday if it means my mother will be okay.

My parents both agree I can stay home from school today. The truth is I don't want to leave my mother's side ever again. My father feels the same way so he also decides to call in sick, which he never has before.

The three of us camp out in the living room watching old 80's movies. We curse at the TV as Molly Ringwald picks Blane over Duckie in Pretty Pink, but that's only after laughing like crazy over the things people thought were cool to wear in those days. All three of us say every line out loud that Judd Nelson gives in the Breakfast Club, and we all decide Long Duck Wong is the best character in Sixteen Candles. My father rolls his eyes as my mother and I swoon over John Cusack in Say Anything.

It's turning out to be a perfect day, except for all the phone calls and texts I'm getting from Nash and Britney. I'm not ready to talk to either one of them yet. I'm not ready to explain what's going on. I think I'm just afraid if I say the words, it'll make it more real than it already is.

I want to keep ignoring them, but the last text from Britney scares me. **"Emma please meet me after school. We really need 2 talk it's about Nash. Please."**

I finally text her back, **"K. Meet me at the front of the school."** I turn to my parents and ask them if I can use their car to go and talk to Britney. I'm scared they are going to say no, since I'm still not sure if I'm grounded for staying out all night. Wow, that night seems so long ago yet it was only two days ago. I really should go speak to Nash too.

"Okay, but we trust you're not heading to see Nash," my father says, reminding me he threatened him.

"I'm not this time. But you both have to understand…."

"We do. And we are not saying you can't see him. Actually, we would really like to meet him. Not like the last time," My mother says, grabbing my father's hand.

"Really? Thank you." I give them both a hug and head out to meet Britney.

Once I'm out of my house I start to feel grief enter my heart again. At home I'm safe and it seems nothing can go wrong, but now out in the real world I'm reminded things do go wrong. Things we cannot control.

Stepping out of my mother's car I take a deep breath, and watch it as I release it back into the air. "We missed you in English class," Court says, taking me by surprise. I don't say a word. "Are you okay? How did everything go with your parents?"

"You knew. That's why you apologized," I whisper finally, realizing why he did it.

"They told you. Huh?"

My throat becomes tight as I nod.

"I'm so sorry Emma."

I fall into his arms and immediately begin to cry. Court knowing makes it more real. My mother has cancer. He holds me tight shielding me from the cold weather that seems to want to choke me now.

"I promise you everything is going to be okay. My parents are going to make sure your mother gets the best medical attention there is."

I nod again as my tears drench his black coat.

"Why am I not surprised to find you in his arms?" I hear a voice filled with anger say.

I slowly turn around to see Nash standing in front of us with his eyes narrowed staring at us.

"Nash? This is not what it...."

"Yeah, right. I'm sure it's not," he spits out.

"I don't have time for this." Court steps back allowing the icy air to touch my skin again. "Emma if you need anything just call me," He says, right before he turns around and walks away.

I look over at Nash, whose jaw is as tight as every muscle in his body is. "Hey," I say walking towards him. "Look, that's not what you think that is."

"I'm not too sure of that."

"What? No. Court was just being a friend. There's something I have to tell you." I tuck my hair behind my left ear.

"Let me guess, you wanna tell me that you slept with Court." My stomach falls straight down to my feet. How did he find out? "Did you sleep with Court in the Hamptons?"

"I...I...I wanted to tell you, but...."

"How could you do this to me?"

I take a step closer to him hoping to God he hears me out. "Please let me explain."

"Explain? Explain that you've been lying to me this whole time?"

"I haven't been lying to you."

"You didn't tell me you slept with Court. What do you call it?"

"It was a mistake. I had just found out you kissed Angie and I thought you were still lying to me. I was overwhelmed by everything I was feeling. Court was there for me and one thing led to another. I'm so sorry I didn't tell you," I try to explain.

"Do you know how I felt when Sam told me you had sex with that asshole?"

"Sam told you?" There is only one way Sam Could know, now I understand why Britney needed to talk to me so urgently.

"Yeah. There I was talking about how much I love you and how we don't lie to one another, only to find out you are a liar. How could you do this to me? Do you want to be with him?" He harshly questions me sending cold daggers into my heart.

"No. I picked you. It's always been you. Don't you believe me?"

"Not when you tell me you want me, but still go off and have sex with him?"

"It was a mistake, just like you kissing Angie was a mistake."

"Kissing Angie is a hell of a lot different than you sleeping with Court." He shakes his head in disbelief. "I still can't believe you slept with him. You know how much that hurts? Every time I look at you I'm going to think about the two of you being together. You are not the person I thought you were."

His words hurt, but also cause a flame of rage to begin inside of me. "No, I'm not the person you want you've made me out to be! I slept with Court! And he and I dealt with it. To be honest with you, I didn't even have to tell you. What I did with Court is my private business."

"I can't even look at you right now," he snarls in disgust.

"So don't look at me! I'm tired of this. I don't need this crap right now. There're other things going on in my life, which are more important, like my family. If you can't get over this then maybe we should be over," I bellow, as people start to gather around us to watch our show.

"I don't think I can get over this."

"I'm sorry you feel that way. Then I guess this relationship is over."

"I guess it is," he says, staring at me without an ounce of love in his eyes.

I do my best to hold my tears back. I will not let him see me cry. "Have a good life." I walk back to my car with a small part of me hoping he'll call my name out, but he doesn't. Unlike the last time I walked away from him, Nash does not chase after me. He lets me go.

My chest begins to hurt as heartache begins to consume me. I cannot break down in this parking lot. I will not allow it. I take in quick breaths trying to fight the urge to come undone. "Emma!" I finally hear someone yell. I turn around to see Britney running towards me. "We have to talk."

"What? You wanna tell me Sam told Nash about Court."

She bites her lower lip before trying to defend herself. "I'm sorry. I really wanted...."

"No. I don't wanna hear it. You got what you wanted. Nash and me are over."

"That's not what I wanted. Sam shouldn't have said...."

"No! You shouldn't have said anything to Sam. That bit of information was between you and me. You had no right to share it with your boyfriend," I spit out with pure anger.

"You're right. Please Emma, I don't wanna fight with you over this."

"Whatever! I don't have time for this right now." I turn around and get in my car. All I want to do is get home and spend time with my mother. She is the only person I want to concentrate on now.

24
Holding On

It's been over a week since I last spoke to Emma. I still can't believe it's over. This is not how it was supposed to be. I'm so mad at her for ruining this relationship. Then again I'm so mad at myself for pushing her towards Court.

"I'm heading to work," my mom says, poking her head into my room.

"I don't care."

"What the hell is wrong with you? You've been a real pain in the ass for the last week. I'm really starting to get annoying. Just tell me what's wrong with you."

"It's not like you would care."

"What's that supposed to mean? Of course I care."

"Yeah right!"

"Does this have anything to do with that girl?" Her face actually looks soft as she asks, making me feel like I might be able to trust her.

"Yeah." It only takes that word for her soft face to turn hard. I knew I shouldn't have said anything. "Damn it. Why did I say anything? Look I know you don't like her, but...."

"Stop right there. I wasn't going to say anything bad. I know I've been against your relationship with her, but that's only because I didn't realize what Angie had done to you."

"Huh?"

"She told me everything. She thought I should know." She comes and sits next to me. "Anyway, I was wrong for comparing you to your father. The truth is I have noticed a huge difference in you since Emma came into your life." I can't believe my mom actually said her name. "She made you smile again." Tears escape her eyes and begin to run down her face. I haven't seen her cry since Ben died. "I'm sorry for never giving her the chance she deserved. Maybe you can bring her over…."

"It's too late. It's over."

"What? Why? Did she do something?"

"No, I did."

"I'm so sorry. Maybe you can…."

I shake my head in agony.

She looks up at me again with pain in her eyes as more tears travel down her face. "I don't want this pain for you. I wish there was something I could do to take this heartache away. I love you." I didn't realize how much I needed to hear those words come out of her mouth.

I lean over and wrap my arms around her. It feels so good to hug my mom again. I've missed this so much. I hug her tighter as my tears now run down my face too. I know where ever Ben is right now he is looking down at us with a smile across his face.

"I love you too mom."

We both start laughing as we pull apart. "Look at us? Who are we?"

"I have no idea."

"Well if you do work things out with Emma invite her over. I would love to really meet her without giving her any of my bitch ass attitude." She walks out of my room leaving me feeling happy and sad at the same time.

Maybe I should try to work things out with Emma. I mean I think I can forgive her. Who am I kidding what we had is over. Both of us have hurt each other way too much. Besides, I'm sure she's already back in Court's arms not thinking about me.

I can't believe how much my heart aches. Why did this have to happen? I'm supposed to be happy with her right now, not missing her like crazy. This sucks.

I need to get out of this house. I walk out of my room and keep on walking until I am outside. Just as I think things can't get any worse a black Mercedes pulls up right in front of my house. What the hell is Court doing here? My fingers curl into my hand to form the perfect fist.

He steps out of his car looking smug. He looks around like he's never seen a neighborhood like mine before. Every inch of me wants to knock him the hell out. He better not be here to gloat.

"What are you doing here?" I snap.

"I need to talk to you."

"How the hell did you find out where I live?"

"Britney told me." I should have known. She's probably happy I'm no longer in the picture.

"Ok, so talk!"

"Why are you doing this to Emma?"

My eyes shoot open. Did he really ask me that? "What?"

"She loves you. Why are you being such a selfish asshole? Get over what happened between Emma and me. It didn't mean anything to her. She needs you right now."

"Is this a joke? I don't get why you're here. Because it sounds to me like you want me to get back with Emma," I vocalize, feeling confused. I must be misunderstanding him.

"That's exactly what I want."

"I don't get it. Here's your chance, why aren't you going after her?"

"Because for some stupid reason she wants you." He steps closer and says, "It was hard to face that, but I did and I'm moving on without her. Look, she needs you right now. Her mom is going in for surgery today...."

"What? Why?"

"Don't you know?"

"Know what?"

"Her mom is sick. She has breast cancer." I can't believe it. I'm such an ass for putting Emma through all this bullshit, while she's going through this. "So you need to get over your stupid issues and be there for her."

I shake my head as I try to process everything he is spilling out on my front yard. "What hospital is she at?"

"Catskill Medical Center. Look, I do need you to know I am going to continue to be in her life. I'm not giving her friendship up for anyone."

"I wouldn't want you to." He begins to walk back to his car. "Yo Court!" He turns around to face me. "Thanks."

"No problem. Just make sure you treat her right."

"I will." I will treat her like she deserves to be treated. She needs me right now, but the truth is I need her too. I run to my truck and race down to the hospital.

I run into the hospital with my heart beating so fast I swear it's going to take off out of my body. After being asked a million questions from the front desk I run towards the elevators.

It's pure torture waiting for it. I have no idea what I'm going to say to Emma. I'm just hoping she'll want to hear me out.

The doors finally open, but instead of stepping in I take a step back. Looking right at me is Mr. Paige. The last time he looked at me that way he was threatening me to stay away from his daughter.

"Are you here to see Emma?" he asks, holding the elevator doors open for me.

"Yeah." I begin to step into the elevator, but stop. It's time for me to do things right. "Actually, Mr. Paige I was wondering if we could talk."

"I was heading for some coffee, would you like to come?"

"Yes." I follow him down towards the coffee shop. I've never felt this scared to talk to anyone before.

* * *

My body will not stop shaking. I hate that my mother in there getting her breast removed. She's only been in there for twenty minutes but it feels a lot longer.

This last week has been a roller coaster ride of emotions. When I'm with my parents I try to act like everything is okay. We've spent every day together. I never thought at sixteen I would want to spend this much time with them.

My mother has been acting like this whole thing is not a big deal. She even makes jokes about being flat chested after the surgery. My father has offered to get her breast implants, which my mother is excited about, and says she wants them to be at least two sizes bigger than the ones she had.

When I'm alone in my room I start to fall apart. I'm so scared to lose her. It doesn't matter how many times they tell me things are going to be okay, it doesn't help soothe my fears. I don't know how I would survive without my mother.

It has helped a little that Britney has been there for me. I chose to forgive her pretty quickly. The truth is, it really wasn't her fault. I should have told Nash about what happened when we first got back together.

Court has also been a great friend. He and Britney take shifts making sure I don't get a lot of time to myself, and bring me tons of ice cream. As much as their friendship has been important to me, I can't help but miss Nash.

I know after what happened I should just leave him in the past, but it's so hard to purge him from my heart. I'm still in love with him and miss him so much. Every time I close my eyes I see his face when he first told me he loved me, but then I see his face full of rage when he told me he knew about Court and me.

"Are you sure you don't wanna go get something to eat?" Britney asks.

"Yeah. I just wanna stay here until the doctor comes out to lets us know how everything turned out. But you can go downstairs if you want to."

"No. I wanna stay up here with you too."

I wish the doctor would come out here already. I don't think my heart can take waiting much longer. "I hope my dad's okay. He's been gone for a while now."

"Maybe he…." We both hear the elevator doors open and whip our heads around to see if it's my father.

My heart almost jumps out of my chest when not only do I see my father walk out but also Nash. What is he doing here? And why is he with my father?

He walks towards me with his golden green eyes focused on me. He gives me a small smile. I want to run into his arms. I want him to tell me everything is going to be all right.

"Hey," he says.

"What are you doing here?" I ask, hoping no one can see how hard my heart is thumping.

"He came to talk to you," my father answers. "Why don't you go talk to him."

"I don't wanna go anywhere until I know Mom is okay."

"Honey, it's going to be a while. Don't worry, I'll be up here and I call you if the doctor comes out with any information."

"Yeah, go. I'll keep your dad company," Britney says giving me an approving smile.

"We can walk around on this floor if you want?" Nash says, taking my hand.

"Okay." As much as my body sings with ecstasy by having my hand in his, I know it's not right. I pull my hand out of his and begin to walk alongside him.

"I'm sorry about your mom."

"How did you find out I was here?"

"Court told me."

"Court?" Why would Court tell him? I don't understand.

"Yeah he came to look for me, and pretty much told me to stop being an asshole and go find you if I really love you." He puts his hand on my arm and turns me to face him. "Emma, I'm so sorry for being such an ass. I let my pride take over. I had no right to judge you after everything I did to you."

"I'm sorry too. I should've been honest with you."

"And I should've been there for you while you been going through all of this with your mom. You are the most important person in my life. You're the person who makes my heart beat faster. The person who makes my stomach do flips. The person I can't wait to see each morning. I'm lost without you. I need you in my life."

My heart melts with each of his declarations. I love him so much, but I also know there has been too much damage done in our relationship. "Nash, as much as I want to jump into your arms, and say everything is going to be okay, I just can't. There's too much that has to be worked out. There's a lot we both have to let go of before we can begin any kind of relationship."

His face falls. "I'm not giving up. I'm going to fight to get you back in life with everything I have."

I smile. "I'm glad. I don't want you to give up either."

"Can I ask you for a favor?"

"Yeah."

"Can I stay here with you? I wanna be here for you."

"I'd like that. I need friends around me right now." He leans forward and gives me a beautiful kiss on the top of my head. I'm not sure if Nash and I can ever get over our issues to be able to be together again, but I'm glad he's here for me right now. "Can I ask you a question?"

"Anything."

"How did you get my dad to be so nice to you?"

"I had a talk with him."

"About what?"

"I pretty much apologized for being a jerk, for not going to talk to him about how I hurt you, and mostly for not respecting his rules. I told him I love you and want to date you with his approval."

"What did he say?" I ask.

"He said he would talk to your mother about having me over for dinner. I hope I can still come over, even if it is just as a friend."

"Of course. I would like that."

"Good. And then maybe the next day you can come to my house for dinner."

"What about your mother?" I ask. I really do not want to start World War III with her.

"Who do you think invited you over?" He smiles. This is all too much. Our parents finally are trying to accept our relationship when there isn't one. "Then I'll be there. Um…do you mind if we head back now? I really want to be there when the doctor comes out to speak to us."

"Of course." We both begin to walk back. This time I allow him to hold my hand.

We arrive just as the doctors finish talking to my dad. My father is leaning against the wall as if he needs it to hold him up. He is as pale as a ghost and tears are running down his face. I let go of Nash's hand as my heart and stomach free fall to nowhere. Oh God, please God don't let anything have gone wrong with the surgery. I run to my dad's side. "Dad?"

"Everything went well. She's in recovery right now," he says taking me in his arms.

I hug him extra tight. "You scared me when I saw you crying."

"Yeah, well I guess I was more nervous than I thought."

"When can I see her?"

"In a couple of hours. Why don't you go get something to eat with Britney and Nash," he says wiping his eyes.

"I don't wanna leave you."

"I'm fine. Please go."

I nod. "Dad?"

"Yeah?"

"She's gonna be okay? Right?"

"Yeah, I'll make sure of it." He smiles. I give him another hug before heading down to the cafeteria with Britney and Nash.

All three of us stand in the elevator not saying a word. I wish there was a way to bring some form of peace between them. There has to be a way to make Britney forgive him the way I have.

"Hey Brit," Nash says smiling, taking me by surprise. "Thanks for letting Court know where I live."

"No problem. I'm just glad you came." I look over at Britney. She winks as a smile comes across her face. She is one amazing friend. I'm so lucky to have her in my life.

Walking into my mother's hospital room frightens me. It breaks my heart to see her laying there with machines hooked up to her. She opens her eyes and smiles.

"Mom, I'm here." I rush to her side and hold her hand close to my heart.

She tries to laugh. "Ouch that hurts."

"Why are you laughing?"

"Because you're wearing a pink shirt."

I also start to laugh. "I love you mom."

"I love you too."

Epilogue
Six months later:

The bell rings and I sprint out of my seat. I have a lot to do before tonight. I'm so happy my parents are allowing me to leave school earlier.

"Hey, you ready to party tonight?" Court asks me putting his arm around my shoulders.

"Yeah, I'm actually excited. I never in my life thought I would be going to prom."

"I know. What's happening to you? First homecoming and now prom, I bet next year I might even see you at pep rally."

"Don't count on it." I laugh. "Well I better go get started on my day of beauty."

"I'm sure you are going to look beautiful," Court says with his gorgeous smile, making me blush.

"Thank you,"

"Hey guys," Britney says, joining us.

"Hey," both Court and me say.

"So Court you ready for prom?" She asks.

"The question is, are you ready for my dance moves?"

Britney and I both start laughing. We both remember Court's horrible dance moves at homecoming.

"Well, I better get going. I'll see you tonight," he says, giving each of us a hug good bye.

"I still wish you were getting ready at my house," I say, as we walk towards my new car.

Yes, my parents finally took me car shopping, and I'm the proud owner of a 2005 black and white Mini Cooper. She is the cutest car ever. I've named her Pixie.

"Me too, but my mom really wants me to get ready at home so she can be part of everything," she says opening the car door.

"Will Mila be there too?"

"Probably. Now that Johnny is home from school we see her almost everyday."

"It's weird to know Johnny is in love."

"I know even though they claim they're just friends. Well, let me go inside and start to get pretty for tonight," she states, as I pull up in front of her house.

"Okay, I'll see you in a couple of hours."

"Bye." Britney hops out of my car and runs inside her house. I'm not sure what I would do without her in my life. She is my rock. After Jason died she became the only friend I could really turn to. I hope we stay in each other's life forever.

Getting ready for prom is actually taking me longer than I thought. I got my nails and toes done, thanks to my dad who treated me. And then I went to get my hair professionally done this time. At first I wanted to do it myself, but now I'm glad I didn't. It actually came out really cute, with big bouncy barrel curls.

Now when it comes to putting on make-up I still suck. I'm having a battle with an eyelash curler and I'm afraid to say its winning. I've pinched my eyelid twice.

"Emma," my mother says walking into my room.

"Yes."

"You look absolutely beautiful." I can't help but smile.

It's been a month since she ended her chemotherapy. She did end up losing all her hair and had bad nausea with it, but my mother was very strong throughout the whole processes. She never once complained. She truly is my hero.

"I'm so glad you picked that dress. It looks perfect on you." She's right, it is perfect because it's a combination of the both of us. I wanted to get a pink dress in honor of her, but she insisted I get a black one, since she knows it's my favorite color. So I decided on a black and pink strapless long A-line empire waist chiffon dress.

"Me too" I say, spinning around. When I turn back to face her I notice she's on the verge of tears. "Mom! You promised me you would not cry."

"I can't help it." She brings her hand up to wipe her eyes. "You're just so beautiful."

I walk over to give her a hug. I close my eyes and try my best not shed some tears too.

"Emma, you're date is here!" My father calls up the stairs.

"Well, we better get down there."

I walk out of my room with every single butterfly in my stomach twirling in bliss. I'm excited to go to prom with the perfect person for me. The person who knows me in ways no one else does. The person who makes me smile every moment I'm with him. The person who takes my breath away each time I see him.

I look down the stairs and feel my legs go weak when I spot Nash standing at the bottom of the stairs dressed in a tux. His golden green eyes look up at me as he forms his crooked smile, I love so much. He's the person my heart belongs to. The person I hold on tight to.

About the Author

Maria E. Monteiro was born in Chile, but grew up in Sleepy Hollow, New York. She now lives with her husband and cat in the Catskills. When she is not writing, she is heading to a concert. Her passion for writing and music go hand and hand. Maria is currently working on Facing Home, an adult romance. Here other book:

Hold on Tight

17158912R00140

Made in the USA
Charleston, SC
29 January 2013